Sweet
MERCY

A NOVEL

OTHER COVENANT BOOKS
BY Donald S. Smurthwaite:

Road to Bountiful

Sweet Merciful Christmas

DONALD S. SMURTHWAITE

Sweet MERCY

A NOVEL

Covenant

Covenant Communications, Inc.

Cover image: *Wishes in the Meadow* © Robert Duncan. For more information, please visit www. robertduncanstudios.com. *Granny's Quilt* © MBCheatham, iStockphotography.com.

Cover design by Christina Marcano © 2018 by Covenant Communications, Inc.

Published by Covenant Communications, Inc.
American Fork, Utah

Printed in the United States of America
First Printing: March 2018

24 23 22 21 20 19 18   10 9 8 7 6 5 4 3 2 1

ISBN-13: 978-1-52440-303-4

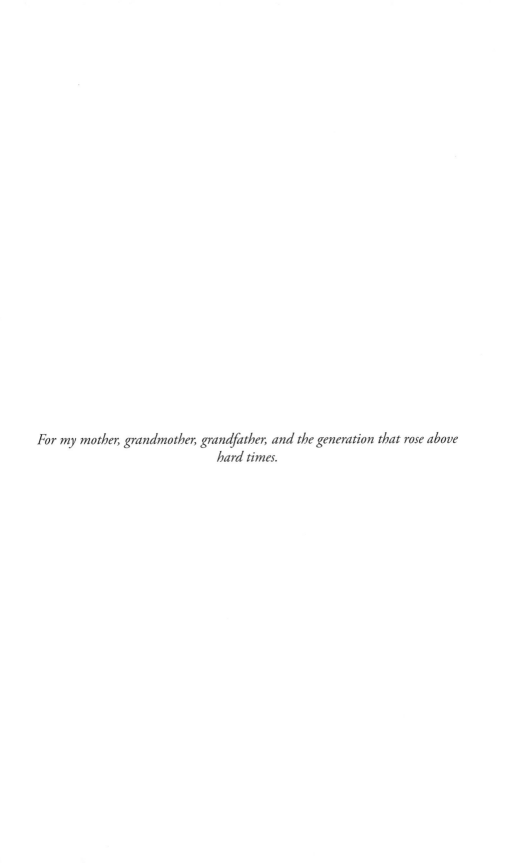

For my mother, grandmother, grandfather, and the generation that rose above hard times.

Acknowledgments

THANKS TO MY SISTERS, SUSAN Hardin and Carol Young, my brother Thomas Smurthwaite, and Richard Nipper, my uncle, for their help in recalling and collecting stories from my mother's childhood. Thanks, too, to the people at Covenant Communications for giving second life to a generation that is now almost gone.

Chapter One

On a pearly skyed spring day, in a small stone house hugging the Snake River rim, egg-bellied Mary Bell stands bent in her kitchen, kneading floury bread dough, and feels the tea-colored stream trickling down the insides of her thighs. "Oh, not now," she groans. "I've too much to do." She is not given to complaint, and that, in the kitchen, with a baby dropped and sliding toward light, is as close to protest as she ever utters. She calls to her six-year-old son Lucas, quietly playing with a splotchy one-eyed kitten on the front porch, and tells him to get the horse and ride to the neighbor's lambing shed and find her husband, Arthur. The message she directs Lucas to deliver is plainspoken: "Come home, Daddy. Mama says the baby is coming. And she says to *hurry*; she doesn't think the baby's gonna wait much more."

The boy runs to the barn, finds the horse named Jenks, and rides three miles to the lambing shed, where he spots his father hunched over a ewe, tending to her needs. With seriousness beyond his years, he delivers the news. Arthur thanks his son and allows himself a slow, small smile. Arthur, the best hired man Scrappy Burroughs has, looks over to his employer on the other side of the delivery chute, nods, and says, "Need to go now. Mary says the baby's coming." Scrappy, who heard the news as Lucas spoke it, is the father of six stout sons. He returns the knowing nod and wishes Arthur luck and silently calculates what he'll do to make up for his leaving the remainder of the day and, if Mary's delivery is not easy, what he'll do for help that night and again tomorrow. Arthur's absence at the peak of lambing season, even for a day, is no small loss. When lambs come, they come, and there's nothing better than having good sheepmen nearby.

Red-eyed, creases in the forehead, gray and grizzled whiskers, sagging shoulders, and smelling of dirt and straw and sheep manure and new birth, Scrappy pouts over the bad timing of it all, but only for a heartbeat. *The bringing forth of a baby. Well now.* That's something he'll just work around. He tells himself that Mary seems a strong young woman and her last delivery was swift with no complications. And then he smiles and thinks of the irony. Either way, Arthur's going to be around new life, no matter what—baby lambs or a baby boy.

Arthur wipes his hands on a rag and brushes straw and grime from his overalls and moves toward the shed door. Scrappy calls out with the mildest of voices, "Give Mary our best. Good luck to ye both. Juanita and I will be over by-and-by, when Mary's up to company. I'm sure you'll be holdin' a new squawkin' son before nightfall."

And Arthur says back, "We'll let you know," and thinks about the arrival of his new boy.

Arthur's logic is this: He is already the father of four boys. He has a primitive faith, a natural belief that in a hard life, in a hard place, when food is scarce and money often a stranger, that God Himself will bless him only with boys. On this point, Providence and Arthur Bell are in complete harmony. Look at Scrappy Burroughs. Six sons. Add to that his own four. *This windy, sage-brushy place and the times themselves demand boys*, Arthur believes. Boys to work the land, boys to watch after the stock. Boys to do all kinds of chores. Boys to bring in the harvest, boys to fish and hunt with, boys to crack the ice in the trough when a bruising, cold January clutches these southern Idaho plains. Boys are riches in these tough times. Boys could mean survival.

And someday, boys of his own to watch out for him and Mary, when their hands tremble and their joints crack and creak and their movements slow and there is little grace in their step and the beauty of their faces is cut by crinkles and sunspots. Boys, in short, to take care of them as they age and wither and sorrow and grow wise and then fall in peace and grace to their final rest and the earth receives them again.

So a son it will be, Arthur decides. A son, taken for granted. Not that he had anything against girls. He fell in love with one, after all, and married her too.

Sturdy in build, thick of torso and legs, his stride short, straight, and purposeful, he quickly climbs onto Jenks and rides in pair with Lucas back to the house, almost as if the old horse was blown along by a stout west wind. Lucas jumps from Jenks and runs ahead of Arthur into the house and then comes out again, determination and fright both plain in his eyes, as his father dismounts and shuffles to the porch. Arthur steps through the doorjamb, squinting, his eyes not accustomed to the dark. "Mary," he calls. "Mary. I'm here."

And Mary Bell sways with effort toward the door and says, "I am ready, Arthur."

He says, "I'll send Lucas for 'Lisabeth. Are you doing all right?"

She smiles wanly and looks at her swollen feet, her puffy, protruding belly, her thick hands and ballooning ankles, and wonders why men ask questions of a stupid nature at times such as these. "Yes. I'm fine. I'm all right."

She looks around the house as Arthur moves toward her. Mary decides when 'Lisabeth arrives she will be in the southwest corner of the bedroom, not the southeast corner, where she has given birth to her last two sons. "You can move the bed to that corner." She motions to Arthur, who looks at her quizzically but wordlessly follows her instruction.

And Mary thinks, *Another little boy. Arthur needs boys. But I wonder.* She waddles to the door then sits on a chair on the porch while Arthur pushes the bed into place. She looks across the flats, away from the rim of the Snake River, toward the Jarbidge Mountains on the southern horizon, still caped in snow, shimmering in the first warmth of the season. She winces at the stabbing stretch of white-hot pain as another contraction pulses through her body. *A little boy. A boy. A little boy will be fine. But I carried different this time, was sicker early on. Maybe there is a surprise in this body of mine. Oh, how I long for the company of a girl in this lonely place.*

She thinks more, *If I move to another side of the room to have this baby, maybe it will be a girl. I need to do something different.* Then she smiles at her own stubborn superstition, and when Arthur emerges from the bedroom and tells her the bed has been moved and all is in place, she grimaces and pushes herself up from the chair and scuttles inside and slowly sinks onto the sheets, and though it is a warm day, she pulls the quilt to her chin and sighs.

Arthur asks, "Do you need anything else? Can I do anything for you?" and she shakes her head *no* and waits for 'Lisabeth, the prim, precise, English-born, seventy-something mercy-angel of the plain, to arrive. If Mary is fortunate, Dr. Poulson will get word and might even arrive in time for the birth. But a woman can depend on 'Lisabeth—Dr. Poulson, not as much. He covers one county and part of another. When delivery time comes, women want 'Lisabeth, trained or not, nearby. She has, after all, given birth to seven children of both kinds. Dr. Poulson, graduate of a fine western medical school and a dozen years in practice notwithstanding, has not yet given birth, nor is he ever likely to.

This is the way women on the Idaho Plain give birth: in their homes. In a room, sometimes with a midwife or a trusted and experienced friend such as 'Lisabeth. Sometimes with a husband there, sometimes with a husband away. Not every boss understands things as well as Scrappy Burroughs. Not every husband understands these things as well as Arthur.

Maternity hospitals are so far away: one in Twin Falls, another in Boise. A small one in Buhl, but the women are leery of it. And, truth be known, the plains-women mostly prefer efficient and calm 'Lisabeth. A few years ago, Mrs. Walter Flynn went to Twin for the birth of her baby; when she returned, the baby was fine and so was she, but Mrs. Flynn complained of being made to stay in bed longer than she wanted and of starchy plain food. "There were things to be done, and they wouldn't let me," she said. "I am not the kind who needs to be pampered. I am not that kind of woman. And the bill. Almost fifty dollars. Far too much for what we got." And what they got was Walter and Bess Flynn's third girl.

Arthur takes his place on the lowest front porch step and sits down and begins to fret. James Richard, barely fourteen months old, is sleeping in a smallish oval metal trough, once used to water stock, now used in amiable mix partly as bassinet, partly as bathtub for the boy, and only occasionally for watering animals. Samuel, the five-year-old, wordlessly approaches and sits beside his father, followed by three-year-old Silas, who flops down on the other side of Arthur. Lucas, his mission to 'Lisabeth's home completed, returns with only a quick nod and takes his rightful place as eldest son, edging in and squatting on his father's right side.

They are a picture, these four: Arthur, Lucas, Samuel, and Silas. Each dressed in overalls. Each sitting, head propped by a cupped right hand, eyes down. Arthur sighs and aimlessly draws a pattern in the dust with his left hand. Lucas, Samuel, and Silas sigh and aimlessly draw patterns in the dust with their left hands. Arthur leans back and puts his hands on his knees. Lucas, Samuel, and Silas mimic him. Arthur stands up and turns in a slow circle, his glance pausing for a moment on the southwest wall of his home, where, only a few feet away, his wife, Mary, is about to bring another soul into the world. His sons, like shadows in early afternoon, do exactly as their father does, although without the anticipation and gravity that Arthur feels.

Arthur puts his hands in his pockets and paces along the creaky wood porch. Lucas, Samuel, and Silas join him in parade a few steps behind.

'Lisabeth arrives, dropped off by a neighbor in an old truck, brisk and business-like, and blows by Arthur and the boys. She dismisses them with a quick look and only says, "Stopped by Jo Powell's on the way in and called the doctor. He should be here soon enough. Now, the four of you stay out here. And Arthur Bell, do not leave James Richard in that trough. It cannot be good for him. Heaven only knows what's left in there. You should know better, young man."

And she bustles into the house, leaving in her wake cold English air and an aura of authority and invincibility. So the man Arthur and his sons wait. And wait some more.

And thus it goes for an hour, then two. For Arthur, it is a difficult thing. Waiting. Waiting, especially when there is work to do. And wondering if Scrappy

Burroughs will dock him pay for time away from the lambing shed. And if he does, Arthur will not begrudge him. He gets paid for being on the job, not for being away, even attending to a wife ready to give birth.

Dr. Poulson arrives. He is younger than Arthur. Tow-headed, bright-blue eyes behind rimless wire spectacles, tall and graceful in movement. Yet the strain of being the only physician trained in obstetrics in a county-and-a-half tells on him: perpetual dark circles under his eyes, slumped shoulders, a weary-of-the-world expression etched on his face, the first strands of silver appearing above his temples. Three more years in southern Idaho, and he will move to Salt Lake City and open a practice there, and a generation of newborn boys will be named Mitchell in his honor, and he will become somewhat wealthy and entirely respected and revered, yet he sometimes will long for those simple, hard, rewarding, and occasionally brutal years on the Idaho Plain, where he learned the most about his trade and even more about the way of people.

Arthur rises and stands on the third step of the porch, his boys all around him, the three of them assuming a mirrored posture: hands plunged deep into their pockets, a look on their faces of part relief, part curiosity. They watch as Dr. Poulson clambers out of his Ford.

"Afternoon, Arthur."

"Same to you, Mitch."

"How is she?"

"Don't know. Okay, I guess. She hasn't said much. Water broke though."

"I'd better go in and see. Elizabeth already inside?"

"Yep. She got here more than an hour ago. She's a quick old gal, that 'Lisabeth."

"Good. I know the ladies like to have another female with them. It's easy insurance to have Elizabeth here in case I could not be available. She knows what she's doing too."

"Yep. That's most certainly the case," Arthur says in his soft Tennessee drawl.

"See you in a bit. I'm sure Mary will be fine. She's strong. But if this," and he pauses, pulls at his collar, looks south toward the mountains, wondering just how best to broach a tender subject. "If this happens again, she really ought to see me more than once or twice before the birth. It helps me to know the history of the pregnancy. It helps her too. It's about the baby and the baby's health and what's best. I won't charge you for those visits." And he winces at his last words because he knows Arthur Bell is a proud man. But the women need a doctor's care.

It is a perpetual problem for Dr. Poulson. These countrywomen who are expecting. They come to him to get confirmation they're pregnant. They meet him on the street or in a store or at church six months later and ask him how they look, and he says they look well but they ought to come in and see him sometime, and they nod and murmur, "yes," and then he usually doesn't see them again until delivery. He understands he is wandering into a tangled thicket that involves pride and independence and strong wills and the desire not to be treated as though they are special or different in any way. And there is the money part. He has taken eggs, pigs, chickens, and promises of labor for payment, and he has taken nothing at all for payment too. But he wants to see expectant mothers more than once at the beginning and again at nine months and four days. He thinks, too, of the babies he might have been able to save if only he were given the chance. And he mourns for them and their mothers and fathers, but mostly the mothers, and he diligently attends the simple services for the babies, although he dreads doing so. He is a good man, this doctor.

"We'll see," Arthur says. "I don't know. Times aren't good. Maybe this one will be our last."

Doctor Poulson lifts his medical bag and starts through the doorway.

"Are you going to deliver me another boy, Doc?"

The doctor laughs out of politeness. It's a joke he's heard a hundred times in his young career. He has a pat answer. "No guarantees. But we'll see what we can do." With that, he enters the house and enters another world altogether. Elizabeth is happy to see him. He smiles confidently and asks Mary about her contractions, and she says every so often, though she is flushed and her eyes register pain. Then he quickly and quietly begins his duties.

And Arthur stays on the front porch as ordered, with a particular feeling, as helpless and alone as a man can be when his wife is only feet away and about to deliver. He feels responsibility and guilt—it was, after all, his doing, the pregnancy—and he worries about feeding another child and the expenses that go along with that. Hand-me-downs help, the big garden is invaluable, and the government has a program that pays for new shoes, but money is scarce, and face it, even those who are doing all right—the Scrappy Burroughses of the world—are only one, maybe two drouthy years or a price crash away from ruin. Lucas, Sam, and Silas, his young companions on this day's wait, soon grow tired and restless and drift away to the back of the house to play marbles in the dirt. James Richard continues his deep nap in the trough. Arthur is alone. He looks across the plain, east to west, at the mostly flat country. He smells the fresh earth turned over, the dampness in the soil, the sense of tender green renewal the land is about to experience. And standing there on his porch, he admires all he can see and he appreciates it, he drinks it all in, and the land almost speaks to him. You either know the land and understand it and love it, or you see the land as just ground, not a place. To Arthur, it is much more than a mere place. His thoughts are tangled and diffused. And so the time passes.

Inside the house, Mary is close, so very close.

Elizabeth stands near Mary's head and says, "Good, Mary, good. Push, my dear. Push a little more. Oh, I know how it hurts. I know. But think of your baby. The worst is here, and the worst is almost over. Good, Mary. Good. You're doing ever so well." And she holds Mary's hand and rubs her forehead, and when the pain is intense and Mary digs her fingernails into Elizabeth's hand, Elizabeth says nothing, except, "Good, Mary, you're doing fine."

And Dr. Poulson says, "A little more, Mrs. Bell. Almost done. I see the baby's head. Dark hair. Your baby has dark hair and plenty of it," and through flashy pain, Mary is cheered.

Outside, Arthur hears the muffled cries of Mary and the low humming of encouragement and instructions from Dr. Poulson and Elizabeth to his wife. Then comes silence, and the sick feeling that something is wrong wells up in him, and though not an overtly religious man, Arthur mumbles a crude and rushed prayer, asking that everything will be all right with his wife and his boy and the others who are helping just on the other side of the stone wall.

Then the world stands still for a second, as though nature is honoring the moment, when from one human life comes another; when one becomes two; when an infant takes its first breath; when the same infant opens its eyes to a blurry, bright, and dry world nothing at all like where it came from; when the rush of air bellows forth from its lungs and the first cry comes. Pink and wet and wrinkly and hairy and hungry, the infant comes from one place to another it has never seen until that instant, and it is a birth in a thousand ways, not just one.

Mary pushes hard, and Elizabeth lovingly says, "You're done, my dear. The baby is here, my love."

Doctor Poulson expertly does what next needs to be done: the fluids suctioned away, the cord cut, the remainder tied, the check from top to toes, and the final pronouncement, "Your baby appears completely healthy, Mrs. Bell. Congratulations on your baby . . ." and he hesitates.

And what is, what is, what is the gender of the infant? Arthur so wants another son. But a daughter. Just one daughter to hold, to dress, to braid her hair, to provide song, to share secrets, to remove, if only temporarily, the trappings of this hard life simply by her sweetness, femininity, presence, and glory. A hazed vision of spring flowers, yellow and blue, a young girl in a white dress sprinting across the meadow flit through Mary's mind.

Dr. Poulson nods at Elizabeth. *A remarkable young man he is*, she thinks. He stands aside. Elizabeth takes the babe in her arms and gently places it on Mary's breast.

And the words she longs to hear, the words formed before only in her own quiet thoughts, the words she desperately wants uttered—all of these words come true, because sometimes the words we want to hear are spoken and not blown away like cut weeds in a sere desert wind. It is Elizabeth who speaks them: "Mary, you have a little girl."

And Mary, through grabby pain and salty tears, can only think of only two words: "Sweet mercy!"

And then Mary, her hard work over and rewarded, asks for a favor, something she is not accustomed to doing. "May I have a sip of water? I'm awfully thirsty."

And later that evening, when Arthur is by her bedside on the southwest corner of the room, Elizabeth hovering close by, Mary tells the story and what she says when she knows the baby is here, safe, and healthy. She says the words again. It is Arthur who tenderly looks at his wife and, with what feels like wisdom and feels like playfulness, says, "That settles it. That's the answer. We have a name for our little girl. Mercy. May. Bell." And Mercy May Bell she is.

Of Arthur it is said, in a story now three generations old, that it took him a bit of time to adjust to being the father of a daughter, but he is a tenacious and honorable man and makes the transition. "A bit of time" translates to about fifteen seconds. Arthur, it seems, was destined to have a daughter in his life, foreordained to sire a girl. The father of a girl is more complete than a father of boys only. Arthur is a quick and steadfast convert. "Anyone can have a boy," he says, with only mild mirth. "But it takes a real something to have a girl."

In the southwest corner of the house on the plain, within a stone's throw of the Snake, Mary nurtures the baby and drifts in and out of light, pleasant sleep. It is a cloudless, gentle day, with a fair wind blowing on the uplands from the Snake River. The spring songbirds are out and happily warbling. The first of new green growth, urged on by a warm sun, nudges its way through a crusty, cloddy earth. The fall and winter rain and snow fell in abundance and the farmers spread all across southern Idaho are quietly optimistic about good crops ahead, though they are loathe to say it aloud. Hope and tender green shoots grow together companionably.

It is a day when the earth itself seems to pivot and swing from one orbit to another, if you are Arthur Bell. If you are there this day and if you know where to look, this is what you'll see: an itinerant farmhand named Arthur sitting stunned on his porch and wondering what he must learn to be a good father to a smidgen of a daughter. At that moment, the entire universe is jumbled and magical, and he can only lay hold of three things: he is the father to a nipper of a girl, he named her, and now he must rear her. It is a bright day for him, as bright as daydawn breaking on the First Resurrection. A new birth, a new story, nudge their way into being.

And that is the story of how my mother, Mercy May Bell Clement, came into this life.

It is April 13, 1925.

Chapter Two

Another day, another place, ninety years later.

It is November, and all that goes with that solemn month is on display: the slant of the sun, the pearl-gray sky, the smell of sodden leaves wet from the western Oregon fall rains. Where verdant crops grew weeks before, only decomposing stubble remains; muted yellows, variegated grays, and faded browns. The sense that the world is falling, falling asleep slowly, and that a giant gray wool blanket is being pulled over it. Every living thing seems in need of a rest.

Mercy May, snowy-haired and frail, now approaching ninety-three years of age, is among those who need rest. She sleeps lightly, propped up in her chair. She lives in the Santiam Lutheran Retirement Center, in a small town just outside a large city. From her big south-facing window, she can see her droopy rhododendrons and bristly rose bushes. Beyond, a grassy lawn, stunted and tawny at this time of the year; the picked-over community garden; and in the distance, an ancient grove of solemn, craggy-barked Douglas fir trees.

She is treated well at the retirement center. The food is plentiful and good enough. The nurses regularly look in on her, their cheerfulness unremitting. The staff seems to know her name; the teens who serve the food are polite and respectful and, sometimes, playful.

I overhear a conversation. Two men, both in wheelchairs, side by side, waiting for their evening meal. Wheezy, croaky voices, dry as a reed in a wind, dewlaps hanging from thin jaws.

"He's been gone two weeks. How I miss him. More than I thought. More. More. Do you know?"

"Yes. I know. I miss him too. Bill, you're about the last friend I have here. You can't go too. You just can't. You're all I have."

"I won't. I can't. I'll try not to. But one of us will go first. Someday."

And then one man reaches out his hand and grasps the hand of his friend and little belled tears run down their faces.

It was the custodian who found Mercy May slumped over in a lobby chair three years ago, newspaper on her lap, slack-jawed, a little after the evening meal ended. Within minutes, she was on her way to the hospital. The stroke would have been fatal, most likely, if it had occurred at night in her room, when no one would have noticed something gone wrong until the morning. The simple thought and act of wanting to read the newspaper after supper in a place where she could be seen almost certainly saved her life.

She stirs and opens her eyes.

"Have I been asleep?"

"Not for long."

"I'm not good company. You come from . . ." and she pauses as she searches for the word. "You come from . . . well, you come from somewhere." And she laughs a little. Her own joke. The stroke took away her recall of many words, peeled away and deposited elsewhere layers of memory. Some words have become strangers to her altogether. She thinks of them but cannot remember their meaning, or she sees them in print and she has no comprehension. Markings, gibberish, little more. "Aphasia" is the medical term for it. The letters mean nothing to her now. They might as well be Chinese characters printed on a rice paper scroll.

"Idaho," she says. "You come from Idaho. That's where. You come all the way to visit me, to spend Thanksgiving, and I can't remember where you live now. Didn't you live in . . . in, that other place? Oh, phooey. I can't remember the name of it now."

"Montana."

"Oh, yes. Montana. Now I remember it. You liked it there."

"Very much. A beautiful place. With people to match the magnificence of the land."

She summons her strength and sits a little higher in her chair. "It's nice that you could come," she says.

"I'm glad it all worked out."

"I come from Idaho. But you knew that. I'm an Idaho girl."

"Yes, I knew that. Born a spud, through and through."

She smiles at the thought. "Through and through. Famous potatoes. And I'm one of them."

She laughs at her own cleverness. Sometimes, the words and thoughts come effortlessly.

And then her eyes close again. "Idaho was an interesting place to grow up because, well. Let's see . . . so much to do."

"You've told me that."

"We had much fun. My brothers. They were always good to me and so much fun. But it was hard, too. Hard times. My daddy."

"I know."

She closes her eyes. Outside, the sky has darkened and a light rain splatters against her window. I feel sleepy, too, the miles of travel perhaps catching up to me. Big Canada geese flail and flap and honk southward against the sky. Out in the hallway, I hear the thud, step, thud, step, thud, step of a resident and his walker making his way toward the dining area.

I reach over and pat her hand. She drifts again into sleep and, I hope, dreams of earlier times and life in a stone house, on a small patch of land, and thoughts of old age and retirement homes and strokes that sap the life from her are millions of miles away.

Hard times on that plain, yes. But good times too. In some ways, the best.

Chapter Three

MERCY MAY MEANS EVERYTHING TO Arthur. No slight to his Mary or his four boys, all of whom he loves with his fiber, bone, and being, but his daughter with soft brown curls is the main reason he rises in the morning, the reason he works so hard, the reason for life itself. She is the reason that he steps home quickly after a long day in the fields. She is the reason he feels the sprout of energy as he nears his door, because *she* will be inside. And *she* will run to him, and he will pick *her* up, and he will twirl *her*, and then he will place *her* feet on his feet, and he will whistle a tune, and *they* will dance on the porch.

He never imagined that his life could be transformed this way, that a deep and hidden part of him that had slumbered, that had never been awakened, would come alive with so much vigor. And all awakened by a little girl. When the work is difficult and long and dirty, when he wonders at how hard he must labor for the little he receives, he thinks of his daughter and how he wants for her to have things—a pair of shoes, a pretty dress, to know a life not as arduous and as fragile as it has been for him and Mary and even the boys.

And he comforts himself by thinking, "A daughter will care for me and Mary when we are old." He now understands that daughters are better suited for this kind of tenderness, this kind of protection. He imagines Mercy May saying someday, "He took care of me all of those years, and now I am going to take care of him."

And he sees life as a simple equation: What he has put into it, he will receive back at a time when it is needed. He invests now, and dividends will come later. It all works out. He feels an intricate part of a great balance, the final balance. He understands that part of life.

And he thinks, on occasion, that maybe on April 13, 1925, part of him came alive, and when Mary gave birth, she gave birth to two beings, not one.

He allows himself to feel hope and to feel joy, things hard to come by for a thirty-nine-year-old man from Tennessee with seven mouths to feed;

an almost-empty pocket of prospects, none of them holding much promise; eking out a hardpan existence on the southern Idaho Plain.

And Mercy May, from the time when she can sense how those around her feel, from the time she is aware of the people and things around her, understands that she is beloved and is a bright throbbing light against a backdrop of darkness. And she grows up happy.

She remembers things from her girlhood. Her brothers—Lucas, Samuel, Silas, and James Richard—and how they were good to her, always. How it was not just Arthur who was enchanted by her arrival, but the entire household of men who would walk by her side, run ahead of her, follow behind, float nearby, provide whatever she desired, attend to whatever she needed.

She remembers the outhouse and how frightened she was to trudge there at night, especially in the rattling cold of winter. She remembers how her brothers would take turns escorting her to the backyard and then, beyond a fence, in the pitch-black in the swirling cold wind, silently stand sentry while she took care of business. "They never complained," she would say years later. Never. It could be midnight or three in the morning, two feet of snow on the ground, and they never said anything when she tugged on a blanket to awaken a brother, who instantly knew the purpose of her visit. It was no wonder that Lucas, Samuel, Silas, and James Richard all grew up to be fine gentlemen. They were trained by their little sister.

She remembers playing baseball games on the long summer evenings, when the day's work was done and the sun still hung in the western sky until well past nine. For bats, a short, stout limb from an oak tree. For a ball, well now, there is a story, a story to tell. Samuel, walking near a schoolyard in town one spring afternoon helping his father with an errand, happens to look down into a patch of weeds and spots a baseball, grimy and brown, there for the taking, thatched in the stubble. He stares at it, not believing his good fortune. Obviously, it is a ball long ago given up as lost. He recites the mantra, "Finders keepers, losers weepers," and justifies his quickly hatched plan. He looks around surreptitiously to see if somebody missing a baseball is nearby, and, seeing no one, he puts the cowhide treasure into his jacket pocket and runs as fast as his legs can carry him, back to the wagon where Arthur is just finishing up loading bags of seed. Samuel caresses and cradles the ball inside his pocket all the way on the bumpy ride home.

He quickly calls his brothers and Mercy May to him, and, eyes darting, breath coming in short, hot bursts, he shows them the ball. His brothers gasp with delight and envy the treasure. There will be a game of baseball tonight, a fine game of baseball. And when Samuel falls asleep in the big bedroom upstairs, the baseball, now all his own, is not left in the barn or the yard, but is tucked under his chicken-feather pillow, ready to launch with him into a night of dreams.

That ball lasts three summers before it finally can no longer be stuffed and stitched and made to do for even another inning. It is whacked fiercely and often, into the hardpan of the yard, or arching high against the blue Idaho sky into the corn patch. When the ball is lost, hit somewhere into the weeds or the ditch, it is cause for grave concern, and in that moment, all unite in a common cause: the baseball must be found. And so it is. Lost then found. Lost then found. Over and over, the life of the baseball renewed, reincarnated, resurrected; and with it, the hopes and games of children. The children learn the pattern well. What is lost can be found. Almost always.

No one has baseball gloves; they are far beyond the reach of what a struggling family can afford. You catch the ball with your bare hands, and after a while, you understand how to hold your hands at a slight angle and feather the baseball into your fingers or the palm. And when you throw the ball, you know how to do so in just the right way: soft enough to be caught, not hard enough to be dropped, fast enough to beat the runner to the bag.

Mercy May, as could be expected, becomes a tomboy and, not by coincidence, a decent second baseman too. There is the time in late August when one of the neighbor family's sons, George Jensen, bowls into Mercy May on a close play at second base; buoyant and feisty as she is, she comes out of the collision wailing and red-cheeked and ready to let both tiny fists fly, to the astonishment of George Jensen, who is paralyzed. He does not know what to do with this howling pixie of a banshee bent on revenge, this young girl who sports a scrape on her knee and a beaut of a shiner already beginning to bulge and darken beneath her left eye. He is helpless, an enemy boat becalmed on a still ocean.

Then there is Lucas, eldest brother of Mercy May, toe-by-toe, chin-by-chin to poor George Jensen, who really was only playing hard, not unfairly. Lucas glances at Mercy May, and in one slight brotherly nod lets her know that her fight has become his fight and that it is acceptable, and possibly preferable, for her to stand aside and lick her wounds and let him take care of this matter of family honor. When you take on one Bell, you take them all on, George swiftly realizes. Lucas, Samuel, Silas, and James Richard close in on George, and words are exchanged and shouting ensues, then pushing; and by the time the scuffle is over, George Jensen is the worse for wear and also has a shiner in bloom, and relations between the Jensen family and the Bell family are, to sum, strained mightily.

Arthur listens later that evening to the account of the game and George's disgraceful slide into the diminutive second sacker. He strokes his chin and looks thoughtful, and then he asks Lucas, "Son, do you think he meant to hurt your sister?"

And Lucas shuffles his feet and pulls at one of his ears and says hoarsely, "No, sir. I believe George just wanted to stretch his single into a double. George plays hard. He likes to win. That's what I believe, sir."

"Then you and your brothers need to walk over to the Jensen's place and apologize. And you'd better take a few ears of corn with you too. The Jensens are a good family, and George always seemed a good boy. We don't want this to spill over into bad feelings between us and them," Arthur rules, and then he looks to the ceiling, perhaps in supplication. "We're all too poor to be feuding. We can't afford ill feelings between neighbors. We've all got to get along."

Properly chastened, in the first phases of shame and repentance, the boys begin their lugubrious march to the Jensen home, Silas hanging on to a small burlap potato sack stuffed with a dozen ears of corn. Arthur watches them go from his front porch. The sun is about down for the day. A nice little breeze is coming up from the canyon. It's warm but not broiling enough to ruin sleep. Mary is inside washing the last of the dishes, with Mercy May perched on a small stool at her side, chattering like a magpie about mean old George Jensen.

Arthur smiles and feels a bit of pride and a great amount of fatherly love for raising boys who would go to the defense of their little sister, even if such gallantry might have been overplayed. *They too are good boys*, Arthur thinks. He knows he is fortunate.

Sixty minutes later, the boys return. Spirits, not to mention good relations with the Jensens, seem to once again be in their proper places. Silas silently hands the burlap bag back to Arthur. It is filled with sweet onions from the Jensen garden.

Corn for onions. There is no better indication that all is right again. Food for food in tough times. The games may begin anew, and they do. Less than a day later, George Jensen again plays baseball with the Bells, and not a word, no trace of grudge hanging over from the previous day, is manifested. Forgiveness comes quickly on the plain. Forgiveness and forgetfulness are easier to come by in hard times, when people don't have the energy, the time, or the will to hold on to bad feelings. This does not mean the will to win wanes. When George, who is indeed a talented baseball player and will one day star on the diamond for the local high school, hits one hard and deep and rounds first base, he slows and makes a long and dramatic, wide circle around Mercy May, who stands near the bag with her hands on her hips, her back turned toward him, her eyes fixed with a cold fury on some distant object, and George might as well have been one of ten million small brown-and-gray pebbles washed onto the vast Snake River Plain many thousands of years before when Lake Bonneville split a side and unleashed a flood that may have been contemporary of what Noah and his clan witnessed.

The truth is, the Bell boys and even Mercy May all thought George was a fine fellow, and when they heard he was gunned down on Anzio Beach years later, they grieved and they hurt and then they recalled the story once more, and then, in some way, they all seemed relieved to have that memory and were glad that no hard feelings lingered, no, not even for a day, and by then, all of the Bell family understood that hard feelings are most often stupid feelings. And how they wish George Jensen could join them for one more ball game just to the side of the corn field and that he could hit one far and they could watch him slowly circle the bases, head up, smiling, the look of peace as a halo around his head. And that they could all again savor the taste of sweet onions, a token of friendship and forgiveness on that summer day.

But there is more to the warm days of late spring and summer and into the fall for the Bell children. Money is hardly there; Scrappy Burroughs does what he can, pays what he can, but it is barely enough to get his family by, much less the Bells. Arthur takes on the occasional odd job to make the money stretch further that year, and they are not pleasant tasks that he does—slaughtering pigs, burning out ditch lines, moving outhouses, picking spuds and sugar beets, pulling calves. Yes, times are difficult, times are precarious, and nobody dares to think much beyond tomorrow or maybe a few days, because doing so can only make you worry and worry, can make you sick, and then, if you are Arthur Bell or someone like him, you can't even show up to work, and you don't get paid and nothing becomes better; it all only becomes worse.

You can't take a day off here or there. You can't slow down and hope to stay even. Hours count, except for that last gasp of the day, as the sun sends long shafts of light from the west and they cast the land in a soft, yellow hue.

It's then, when the chores are done, when the work comes to a blessed halt for the family, Arthur and Mary urge and cajole and almost force their children outside for a game of hide-and-seek, kick the can, red rover, or steal the flag. And when their children are all out in the patch of dusty yard, and when they are hiding in the cornstalks and the trees, and when they are calling to each other and shouting and giggling and falling down because they are laughing so hard, it brings a joy to Arthur and Mary as nothing else can. For a moment, there is a respite, a peace from the curse of Adam, the toil of earning their daily bread by the sweat of their brow.

Mercy May, darling of the family that she is, the only daughter, nonetheless learns to work hard and take on chores. No princess is she. From the days even before she enters school, she helps Mary with the wash and cleaning the house. She knows what a callous on her hand and a blister on her foot are before most town children know how to tie their shoelaces.

The bean patch is her special province. The bean patch is hers, and although her brothers help her plant the beans, after that, the caring and nurturing of the crop falls upon her slim shoulders. She hoes the bean field. She hand-waters when the skies dry up and the water in the ditch doesn't come through, bucket by bucket, from the well to the patch and back again, back and forth a dozen times each day. She watches the beans blossom, sprout, and grow, and then in August, she begins to pick them. The Idaho sun is without compassion; it burns hot yellow and broils and saps her strength. Her mouth becomes cottony, and she cannot swallow, and her sun bonnet does her little good. Her arms become leaden and her legs ache from the work of picking the beans. Her skin bakes and cracks. The work is not fun.

But work is what she knows, and she understands that everyone in this family must contribute something, even if they are young and small. Beans count, beans matter in the family economy. Raise their own food. It is simply what families do, what they must do to keep going.

And on the cold autumn and winter nights, when the wind screeches in from the west and snow puffs and splatters underneath the door frame and into the house, on those kinds of nights, when Mary puts warm beans mixed with a little bacon and onion on the table, it all seems worthwhile to Mercy May.

"Beans taste good; you did fine work, Mercy May," Arthur says, slowly chewing the knuckled green vegetable, and those words of praise from her father mean as much to her as any she will ever receive in life. "Mighty good. Fine, fine. Delicious. Good of beans as I've ever eaten."

Food is central; food is the basic reason for what the Bells do each day. It just comes to that. Life on the plain is boiled down simply to putting up enough food to eat when you are hungry. When you are hungry, you don't think about much else, only the gnawing in your stomach and how good it would be to have a nice piece of bread or some berries or some beans with bacon and onion. You can dream of being rich, of living in town, of going to a store and buying what you need, but the dreams don't last long, because your stomach is empty and you have to summon the strength to go about doing what needs to be done to get food. It is not a fancy life, and there are no frills. You must always think about where the next meal is coming from and then the meal after that. You must look ahead a week and a month and plan and economize to ensure there will be food on the table. Arthur knows this, and he feels the weight of responsibility to provide food. More than shelter, more than warmth. It all begins with food.

They have animals. Chickens, cows, pigs, and occasionally turkeys. Mercy May is fond of a little piglet, and she gives him a name that she keeps to herself. She watches over him more closely than the other animals. She gives him a little extra slop when she feeds him, delights in his antics, thinks he is cute, at least as cute as a small pig can be.

Then, on a Christmas Eve in 1929, Mary pulls from the wood-fueled stove a pig for the family dinner. He looks just as he did when she last saw him, baked whole, only brown and dead now, and a curious, mocking smile on his face. Mercy May gulps at the sight, and part of her pulls one way and part of her pulls another, and for a moment, she is confused and does not know what to do.

The air in the little house in fragrant with the aroma of spicy meat. In the middle of the room, a small juniper Christmas tree is propped up by a crude wood stand. A fire blazes in the stove, fueled not by coal or sage grass but by wood, which is counted a luxury for the Bell family.

Arthur stands at the head of the table and pronounces softly but with some pride, "Our Christmas Eve dinner, thanks to the Lord who provides," and her brothers cheer and clap and her mother holds the pig high on the platter, and Mercy May thinks of her empty, growling stomach and her decision is made as a prayer over the food is offered by Arthur, and later she chews the pork slowly and savors its flavor and the gnawing in her stomach is assuaged and, coupled with apple pie, she feels fuller than she has in a long while.

She too thanks the Lord who has provided, although she is not quite sure just what He has done to put the pig on the table. And in this way, this meal of a small pig on a cold December night and other instances like it in her childhood, she becomes practical, which is a trait she will use and treasure throughout her long and useful life. Her philosophy becomes: The Lord can provide if He chooses, and if He makes good, it is okay to partake of His treasure. *It also helps the Lord if everyone chooses to work at things,* she decides.

***

She is awake and sitting in her chair. The television drones quietly in a corner of her small apartment. She refused from the beginning to call this a retirement center or a rest home, and most forbidden of all in the lexicon of the aging, a nursing home. "The resort" is what she calls this place. She enjoys telling people she lives at a resort, and she has been calling it that for so long that part of me wonders if she really considers the long, two-story, L-shaped building a resort.

"I need to get back to Carol's now, Mom."

"I'm sorry," she says simply, slowly. "That you have to go."

"It was nice talking to you tonight. The story about George running over you in the baseball game. And the little pig. You didn't have much. You didn't have anything. It must have been difficult."

"We had enough," she says. "And they were . . . they were . . ." and her mind drifts a little, and she searches for words, words floating out on a sea for which she needs to cast a net and somehow pull in. "They were interesting," she says, settling on a familiar and useful word. "We always got by. People nowadays don't know how to get by. We had to get by. We didn't have much choice. Those times . . . shaped me. And . . ." She pauses and goes off on a momentary journey for words, finds them, and returns. "I can no longer eat . . . pork."

"I'll be by about ten in the morning."

"We'll shop?"

"Yes. We'll shop."

"Good. It gives me something . . . to look forward . . . to."

I bend over and give her a light kiss and wish her good night. Her skin feels like thin paper to my lips. Her hair is white and strandy.

"In the morning," I say.

"Yes, then. I'll see you. He was a cute little pig . . ."

She closes her eyes, and a slight smile sweeps across her features. Where is she? What time, what date, what place? Which thoughts settle; which are cast aside? What sieve do you apply to the events of your life? What do you remember, what is important, what do you simply let go, sand piling on sand, until only the important events and memories are left? After everything has passed through the roaring furnace, the dross cast aside, only gold must remain. The gold is truth, the meaning of your life, the sum of your existence. It must be the truth, unembellished, standing alone, indisputable, unassailable. The truth is gold.

She says, barely above a whisper, "It was that year. The year 1933, when everything began to change. I still remember everything about it as though it was last year. Mother and Daddy; Mr. Burroughs; Mr. Bowker; my teacher, Mrs. Durham; the Andrews boys; my brothers; and . . . all of them. All of them. It was all in 1933, and then came the next spring."

I listen. I say nothing. Her eyes close again and remain closed this time. Her breathing takes on a slow, deep rhythm. My sister, who lives nearby, says that Mother often sleeps in her chair. I place a quilt from her couch over her shoulders and tiptoe to the door.

"Good night, Mother. Good night, sweet Mercy May."

The air is damp and cold and smells of old fir and moist, rotting leaves. I tug my coat collar high and trudge, hands deep in pockets, mind deep in thought, toward my car. I think about generations and how time separates us so little, but other things—and I have a quick lightning vision of a small pig, a macabre smile on his face, carried in on a plate to raucous Christmas Eve cheers—separate us as though we were born and lived in different worlds if not different universes.

Chapter Four

I ARRIVE A FEW MINUTES before ten the following morning. She is not ready. As if I am surprised. She is legendary among family members for her slowness, for dawdling, for taking her time. But she has earned her slowness, and perhaps it's a late-in-life virtue in a world that speeds and tumbles along with so little regard for the present, looking ahead and ahead, more and more, further and further. I think, *We move quickly when we are trying to get away from something, and we move slowly when we want moments to last.*

She wants her moments to last.

Eventually, we make the slow trip down the long hallway, accompanied by the clinking of her walker on the linoleum floor, then to the door with the rectangular green exit sign over it; and finally to the car. We've become good through the years at the routine of getting her into the car: where I position her, the angle of her walker, the quick firm grip on her forearms, the slow pirouette, and the slide into the passenger seat.

I walk around to the driver's side, get in, buckle her seat belt, and we start toward her favorite store: part pharmacy, part variety, part grocery, part unable to be categorized. She will spend ninety minutes walking slowly up and down each aisle, occasionally asking me to reach an object for her and place it in her shopping cart. Patience. Slowness. Deliberate. Purposeful.

Then back to the resort, just in time for lunch. The dining room is mostly cleared out; the young servers have finished most of their work and gather at a table in a far corner of the room, talking, laughing, picking at their food.

Mercy May struggles getting her shrimp salad balanced on her fork. She slowly sips a soft drink. And then, from nowhere or somewhere or anywhere, she holds her head high and says clearly, "Did you know that I've always loved to read?"

***

The magazines from Lollie arrive about every other month, wrapped in brown paper, sturdy white twine neatly cordoning the packet. Lollie is Arthur's older sister, back in Tennessee. She is the one in the family who seems wealthy, wealthy enough to subscribe to several magazines, "women's magazines" they're called, and Lollie is aware enough and kind enough to understand what a treat a used magazine can be to Mary and young Mercy May. Lollie's husband is Martin, and Martin is the postmaster in a small town, and between what she subscribes to and the leftover magazines that are undeliverable that Martin slyly brings home, the small table in their living room quickly acquires mounds of magazines. Lollie, practical like her brother, cannot bear to throw away anything that might be of use, so she diligently stacks the magazines and wraps them and binds them with the twine and sends them to Idaho for her sister-in-law and her young niece, whom she has never met but has heard is bright and active and loves to read.

Lollie has a picture in her mind, and it is a good picture and she feels light inside whenever she imagines it. The picture is this: a small house on a dusty plain in the summer, snowy and cold in the winter, pleasant enough in the spring and fall; and a woman who goes out to meet the postman who comes by twice weekly, is delighted when he hands her the thick package of brown paper, sent from far away; and the woman later sitting side by side with a child in a small kitchen, and they go over every page of every magazine, reading the stories and pointing to the pictures and absorbing it all and feeling gratitude for a relative in faraway Tennessee who is thoughtful and has the money to send these lightly used magazines to them.

And that is the picture Lollie has, and it is a true picture; the woman and the child do sit side by side, often in the fading, flickering light from the fireplace, and not a word escapes and not a beautiful piece of artwork goes unnoticed, and not an advertisement is read without the slight feeling of wistfulness welling gently inside them. And these magazines become their eyes to the world, with the pictures of women in long, chic dresses and suits and beautiful gorgeous hats, and suave and sophisticated men with thin moustaches, jaunty smiles, all of whom look a little like Gable and Flynn. Mary and Mercy May pore over the magazines—*Ladies Home Journal, Coronet, Woman's Home Companion,* the *Saturday Evening Post*—and they cherish the ads for Cream of Wheat and beauty creams and hosiery and Coca-Cola and Mr. Ford's Model T car, the cheapest version costing an astronomical $525.

The mother is amazed at how quickly her child gathers it all in, soaks it in like rainfall on the desert floor in August, and she tells her husband, and sometimes, when he has come home, he asks his daughter what she has read, and she goes into long and detailed stories about her exotic voyages across printed pages, and true to her independent nature, she tells her father what she thinks about what she has read.

And at night, as Arthur and Mary lie in bed, they sometimes talk about their daughter. And they say, "Smart as a whip. Always got her nose in a magazine. Always got something to say. And how she can read! She already reads better than her brothers. And me and you too."

So it is one evening in late summer, when the sun has risen high in the sky and is taking its own slow turn at setting, when the air is hot and thick and the crickets are humming and beetles clicking, Arthur settles into his chair and lets out a sigh, and he notices his daughter with her nose in a book, and he says, "Mercy May, what are you reading?"

"Nothing."

"You are reading something. It's a book. It can't be nothing."

And Mercy May wriggles uncomfortably on the hardwood chair at the kitchen table and says, "Just a book. Aunt Lollie sent me a little book in the mail."

"What's the book about?"

"Poems, Daddy. It's a poem book."

"Poems?"

"Yes, sir. The book is called, 'One Hundred Beloved Poems.'"

"Poems. Hmm. Poems. Don't know many poems." And he sits up in his chair a little more. "Well, then, can you read me a poem? Something with a good rhyme. How about it?"

Mercy May is torn. She is old enough to know that life on the Idaho Plain is not easy, and little in the way of frills or fancies are tolerated. There is no time for them, and more practically, no use for them. They do not put bread on the table nor change in the sugar bowl, the instrument used by the Bell family as a depository. She thinks that poetry may very well be an unneeded trimming and wonders what her father will say, what he will conclude.

He teases, "I'm still waiting for that poem, Mercy May. Something sensible."

And in a heartbeat, she decides. And then she begins.

> *"That is no country for old men. The young*
> *In one another's arms, birds in the trees,*
> *—Those dying generations—at their song,*
> *The salmon-falls, the mackerel-crowded seas . . ."*

And she reads more from Mr. William Butler Yeats, and it is on this night that Mr. Yeats meets Mr. Arthur Bell and a curious yet respectful friendship is formed.

"An aged man is but a paltry thing,
A tattered coat upon a stick, unless . . ."

Arthur, from the hill country of East Tennessee, who has a sixth-grade education but is wise and kind and has an innate empathy for others, stops her. "You say, 'An aged man is but a paltry thing, A tattered coat upon a stick . . .' or something like that?"

"Yes, Daddy."

"And the poem writer is saying that an old man isn't much, sort of like a ragged coat just hung on a stick?" Arthur much prefers the words "poem writer" to "poet," which sounds sissified and flabby to his ear.

"I think so, Daddy. I think that's what he means," Mercy May says cautiously.

Arthur rises from his chair and runs his hand through his hair and looks at the floor and seems to be pulling in thoughts from a million miles away, as if commanding planetary tides from a moon. Mary watches quietly, the slightest of smiles stealing across her features. A small clock on the mantle precisely ticks away the seconds and a robin trills its evening song.

"A tattered coat, just there flapping on a stick," Arthur says, turning toward the one window overlooking the porch. "Worn-out. All in. I've known men like that, men like sticks with an old coat on. I believe that poem writer knows what he's talking about. Can you read a little more, Mercy May? What did you say the name of that poem writer is?"

And a new poetry comes into Arthur's life, one that depends on words. It is beyond the poetry he sees and understands each day: The miracle of the sun yawning and stretching from the east; the wonder of little pale and dark seeds, planted, then sprouting, then growing into what he can put on the table to feed his family; the continual amazement of recognizing he is a father and a husband and that people depend on him, count on him, and that this is, somehow, *his time*; and the verse that accompanies the steady, rough rhythm of his days, working a steady rough land. And, of course, the poetry he sees in every movement and every expression and every word uttered by his last child, the girl Mercy May.

So Mercy May finishes "Sailing to Byzantium," and at the end, Arthur says, "I know what he means. This Idaho. It's no country for old men, neither."

A new star rises in the Idaho firmament. Poetry becomes a Bell household tradition. The boys never find much use for it, but Arthur does. It carries him away, gets him thinking new thoughts, allows him to see places and things for the first time or common things in a different way. Once or twice a week, he sits back in his chair in the evening and suggests that Mercy May read him verse. Not many months pass by before Mercy May, nimble-minded, facile, someone who gravitates toward words the way some people are drawn to a cool sip of water on a scorching day or others seek the warmth of a fire on a numbing, cold winter night, has many, maybe most, of the one hundred best-loved poems in all human history committed to memory.

And the two of them, farmhand and daughter, become cautious yet insightful critics.

Yeats: A good turn of phrase, and he knows people well enough.

Dickinson: Simple words—you can understand what she's getting at, but awful dour. Didn't seem to have much luck with men.

Shakespeare and his sonnets: A little hard to get at his meaning, but he could sure put to use pretty words.

Wordsworth: Now there was a fine poem writer.

Tennyson: Mostly down-to-earth. Might have some farm blood in him.

Keats: Just when you're about to give up on him, he says something that makes a lot of sense, so you should try to keep up with where he's headed, even when he goes flowery.

Arthur never tires of Mercy May's reading or reciting poetry to him. He wishes he had more education and knew words better and had a knack for rhyming; if so, maybe he could write poems too. He thinks, *First one I'd write would be for my girl.* Then he thinks again, *No. I'd write one for Mary. Then Mercy May. Somehow, I'd figure out one for the boys, too, but it might have to be rougher in the words and the meaning. And I'd like to put one on paper about farming and how things grow, seed coming up for the first time, and the way the sun chases away the chill in the spring mornings and what it feels like to work hard and always be tired and never have enough to show for it. That's what I'd do if I could write poems, but I can't.*

He thinks those things not realizing that he has, in his mind, composed a very good poem that is also a true poem, the words as true as when Yeats wrote about sticks and tattered coats.

And from that day forward, if you were with Arthur Bell in the water ditch or taking a ewe and shaving the wool off her, or bucking bales of hay, or crawling under a truck that wasn't running, you might have heard him, quietly, so quietly, murmuring a bit of Wordsworth:

"What'er the theme, the maiden sang
As if her song could have no ending;
I saw her singing at her work,
And o'er the sickle bending;
I listened, motionless and still;
And, as I mounted up the hill,
The music in my heart I bore
Long after it was heard no more."

***

Poems are the closest thing that Arthur and Mary Bell and their boys and their daughter have to luxury during these times. These times, the twenties then drifting into the thirties, past the end of one war, another stealing and grinding toward them. They are hard enough now and about to become even harder.

The people of Idaho had rolled up their sleeves for World War I. The nation needed raw products to support the troops, and Idaho lent a nursing breast; her minerals made to metal, her timber turned to lumber, her water transformed to electrical power by dams on the Snake and South Fork of the Boise, her farms and ranches producing food for a hungry people.

The war brought good times to Idaho, in a way, because the nation needed what Idaho had and needed the people who knew to get out of her what was required. And when the war was over, Idaho was quickly forgotten, a small state with an awkward people, and most of the rest of the nation sprinted ahead into a heady, careless prosperity while Idaho made big arm motions and kicked hard in the water for a time and then slowly wearied and slipped under a rising tide. You talk with people who lived back then and they tell you: Idaho felt the effects of a wrecked economy long before anyone on a busy street in New York City even had the faintest whiff of trouble.

By the time the rest of the nation falls on that dark day in October of 1929, Idaho is already flat on its back in a long tube of a water well, blowing desperate bubbles, looking skyward with no hope.

Nor is Idaho completely spared the dry, windy, and dusty weather experienced in the Texas and Oklahoma panhandles and parts of the country's bread basket, where the good, natural sod is plowed up, reduced to grainy specks, and the wind spews soil twenty miles into the air and then the wind takes it away. The Idaho winter snows are only so-so some years; spring rains only part of what they normally should be. Big streams turn into little streams, little streams broken into a series of puddles. The crops come in all right at the beginning, but the lack of water in the intricate system of canals saps them of their vitality, and the wind dries them, and the sun scorches them.

So the little green shoots and stalks turn yellow, then a sickly tan, and then a crisp, dry, bristly brown. And the wind blows through them and makes a whining sound and a fluttering sound, and the lines of worry etch deeper on the faces of those who know the land best and fear what the next day and week and month will bring.

And along with the crops, hopes begin to shrivel and turn to little more than fine, powdery dust blown away by a searing desert wind. And prices. Prices fall in a way never seen before, so even if the big canals supply you with water, what you get in pay for your crop is so paltry it mightn't have been worth growing anything beyond what your family needs in the first place. Some farmers just let the crops go. No use tending a good-for-nothing crop.

What they dread most is hunger. Just hunger. Not enough in the belly, not enough to sustain a child or a woman or a man. You drag through the day with a hole in your stomach and not enough energy to hardly lift your head or walk to the barn, much less to put in a good day's work for a wage that will only allow you and your family to become even hungrier the next day.

You cannot feel hopeful or optimistic when you experience hunger, true hunger—the kind that never leaves you alone and makes you feel helpless. You can't think much, you can't look ahead, you can't plan for much of anything.

Which is the greatest irony of all for Arthur. He'd come to Idaho with a plan. Work for someone for a few years, live a lean, spare life, and then set aside a stake a little at a time, until he can afford a small place of his own. From there, add to it bit by bit, until the day when he can look out at two or three hundred acres and call it his own and he can feed a thousand people just by what sprouts from his land.

You can't take land away, he thinks, and it is land that provides everything. Arthur loves the land, and his plan is to own as much of it as he can so he can feed his family and, if need be, his neighbors too. Arthur is not a greedy man. He makes good on part of the plan, part of his dream. He had crossed paths with a family of easterners named Roseberry who were ready to pitch it all in and roll over. Seduced by the magazine and newspaper ads, puffy with dreams of verdant land, plentiful water, and certain wealth, and swayed by the swift, slick public-relations talkers from the West, they came to Idaho expecting the place to be cheek by jowl with the Garden of Eden. Then reality hit them: grubbing sagebrush was more the work of Lucifer than of Adam, and they wanted out. The winters were almost unbearable and the summers sticky hot. Dejected, they asked only a thousand dollars for their small plot of land and unfinished stone cabin that was more tar paper lean-to than home. Arthur heard of it and latched hold of every cent he had saved in his thrifty life and offered the fleeing family three hundred and fourteen dollars and fifty cents. John Roseberry extended his hand with palm up, took the cash, bought train tickets, and headed back to Delaware, a bent if not broken man. In a gesture part generous and part hopelessness, he told Arthur to keep anything of value around the hovel and fifteen acres and there was no need to forward the mail back east.

So Arthur had a shack and fifteen powdery acres. He and Mary had their place, had realized the first part of the dream and worked with respectable industry to prop up and improve the shack and make it into a home, a home made mostly of stone hijacked carefully from the alluvial plain. But that is all the further the dream went. The rest of it wilted and died, simply died. It was taken away in part by a merciless sun, the cloudless blue sky, the parching wind, and the paucity of snow in the mountains and, even with the canals, not enough water on the river plain, and the worst beast of all—the deadly downward flush of prices.

And it was also taken away by the greed of people in faraway cities, people he never saw or knew; those who wanted more and got it and then wanted even more and more after that, until the house of cards could no longer bear it and collapsed into a heap. How hard it was to come by money when you were just a farmhand with little education, no matter how hard you worked and how hard you tried to save and set a little something aside. Arthur would never again have as much as three hundred and fourteen dollars and fifty cents to his name.

And seven mouths to feed. My. Seven. How did all of this happen? How did he come to be in such dire shape as this? Oh, he doesn't mind if he goes without, but the thought of Mary or Mercy May or the boys without enough food keeps his eyes open at night, his mind racing through a series of what-ifs and what-abouts until he cradles his temples with his hands in the dark of night, lying in bed, Mary at his side in a light dreamless sleep, and he almost pleads aloud for the freight train to stop screeching between his ears. Maybe John Roseberry had the right idea. Sometimes, you just have to give up and go away, cut your losses. But that is not Arthur.

And at times, this strong, good man quietly turns himself inside out at night and wonders if he can ever find a better way for his family, even if it means giving up on his plan, which is really his dream, and when the morning comes, he rises before sunup, puts on his working clothes, and heads over to Scrappy Burroughs's place and begins his long day of labor. *Your dreams,* he figure, *come quickly and easily, but making them true is a steep, pebbly, and treacherous slope to climb.* Yet he feels, in those rosy and yellow summer mornings before the sun begins to broil, the blinking pulse of hope that just maybe a new day will bring a better fate; maybe something will signal the beginning of a long, slow turnaround.

A few men achieve Arthur's elusive dream. Scrappy Burroughs is one of them.

This is Scrappy Burroughs: a large man, with a big head and rubbery, droopy ears, grizzled hair, craggy-faced, ruddy red-and-white skin cancers spidering over his nose and cheeks. You can hear his call from a field away, and you can hear his booming laugh from a county over. Arthur has known Scrappy Burroughs for nine years, almost from the very day he arrived in Idaho from Tennessee, and Arthur can count the times on one hand he has not seen his friend and employer in his farm garb: big striped blue-gray overalls, brown, scraggy working boots, and a hat, usually a sun-bleached, loppy-brimmed version of a fedora. For several years, Arthur, in fact, had never realized that, save for a fringe of grizzled hair, Scrappy is almost as bald as a melon, until he chanced upon Scrappy leaning over the small intermittent creek that ran through the property, splashing handfuls of cooling water on his face under a startlingly harsh June sun.

But there is more to Scrappy Burroughs than his imposing, big-oak-tree physical presence.

Oh yes, he had his day when he was a wild one who appeared at all the dances and was known to take his hand to cards and whiskey at the Bucket of Blood Saloon, but that side of him dried and blew away like dust once he met Juanita. It was Juanita who turned him around, got him settled and grounded, and helped him to become the man he now is: true. Scrappy is *true*. The word fits his nature. Everything he does is true, is correct, is generous and bighearted. You can count on Scrappy Burroughs. When your fence breaks and you need help to repair it, when a heifer is having trouble in birth, when you need a meaty hand on your shoulder and a word of encouragement, Scrappy Burroughs is there. When you need a few extra bales of hay or someone to help you patch your roof or stop by with a turkey before Christmas, Scrappy Burroughs is there. When a family was down on its luck, when illness slaps the wage-earner of the family, Scrappy is there, moving in and about like a light-quick fog, leaving a basket of food or a few dollars and, maybe most helpful of all, uplifting the spirits of those who need it.

Scrappy Burroughs is a second-generation Idahoan. His father settled on the plain below the Magic Valley in the 1880s and immediately began to buy up land. When the Carey Act came about and the federal government got reckless about almost giving land away, he followed the formula prescribed by the law: claim some land, clear it, build a wood-and-cardboard shanty, plant crops on an eighth of it, and then prove it up before the land commission and it was yours. Foolish government. The Burroughs family prospered right along with the land, growing and harvesting crops, producing a long line of strong, healthy sons, with a few daughters scattered along the way. When the federal government's South Side Irrigation Tract came into being, with its promise of never-ending water supplies and its ability to turn gnarled, arid sagebrush country into fertile farmland, it was as if the Burroughs family struck gold. His father scratched together enough to eventually own one hundred and sixty acres; from that modest beginning, Scrappy cobbled together another six hundred. When Scrappy bought land, he paid a fair price for it. He was not one to take advantage of another's circumstances or misfortune.

He met Arthur in town, at the general store; Arthur was there to purchase a few of the essentials, enough to get his family started—flour, wheat, sugar, cornmeal, coffee, a bit of molasses. Gabe Sperry, owner of the store, asked Arthur if he'd like to open a line of credit, and Arthur said that no, if he didn't have the money, he'd find a way to get along without whatever beckoned.

Scrappy, there hefting a shovel, liked what he heard in that soft, rolling Tennessee accent and took note, as a student of human nature would; in tune as he was with all that took place on his part of the plain, he already knew where Arthur lived. A day later, he and Juanita showed up at the small stone house that Arthur had bought cheap, a pie and cake in hand, and Juanita and Mary right away plunging into wise and sisterly chatter. Scrappy looked at Arthur's strong, scarred, and calloused hands and made a quick and shrewd judgment. Scrappy knew you could tell much about the character of a man by the look and complexion of his hands. A week later, Arthur began working for Scrappy.

Working for Scrappy is considered a plum job on the plain. You know your wages will be fair and you will be paid on time. You know he won't dun you on your hours or charge you if a piece of gear breaks in your hands, even if you are at fault, and if it is a good year, you might even get half-day off on the Fourth and paid a full day's wage for Thanksgiving and Christmas. On your wife's birthday, something he knows about without ever having to ask, he'll send you home early but never do so for your own birthday.

Men look up to Scrappy Burroughs. They seek his counsel and his company. He is the Jeremiah of the plains. His word carries weight, his vision of the future is taken as sure prophecy; his promises are hard steel. He suffers sincere fools well but has little tolerance for fools who knew better. No one in the county knows sheep better than he. And it fits him. He is, in a manner, a shepherd by trade, and he is, in another, the shepherd of those four dozen or so families who live near him as a community on the south side of the river canyon. But things are changing, even for institutions like Scrappy Burroughs. Not even he can escape the effects of dust and little water, the fever of turning natural sod into farmland and watching it blow across the country, of unrelenting sun and wind, and economic doings in faraway places that will eventually settle like a plague on the Snake River Plain and cause even strong men to fall onto their knees with a whimper, the only sign of water the salty tears in the corners of their eyes.

***

Arthur burns weeds from water ditches one spring in 1932, a hard, grinding job. He will come home from ditch-burning days reeking of blue-black smoke, red-eyed, his tongue thick, and his mouth tasting of pungent tar and ash. He moves methodically down the ditch, gasoline-soaked rags on the end of a torch, spreading yellow and orange flame along the way. He sees Scrappy's Ford truck puttering its way toward him. Scrappy stops, gets out, and ambles toward Arthur.

"Mornin', Arthur," he says amiably, but, already from his voice and in his look, Arthur knows Scrappy is dealing with devils inside. "Good day for burnin', you think?"

"Yep. Good day for it. Not much wind. Weeds aren't too thick here," Arthur says.

"Family?"

"Well enough. Good as far as I can tell."

"Nice to hear."

Scrappy scratches the back of his neck and takes a bandana and wipes his forehead. He raises his left foot and scratches his right foot with a heavy working boot. He looks at Arthur as though there is something he wants to say but can't reach out and pull the right words in. Arthur understands his employer, his mentor, his friend. Arthur makes it easy on Scrappy, as easy as it can be. Arthur knows what is turning around in Scrappy's head, what churns and whirls inside. In bad times, in hard times, workingmen know. They just do.

"Need to say something to me, Scrappy?"

"Well, maybe. I do. I need to say something to you, Arthur. I do."

Arthur tosses his torch into the ditch, the part of the stubbly gully that has already burned. He stands square up to Scrappy and puts his arms to his side, hands down, not crossed. His posture is such that it says, *I'll listen to what you have to say, and I won't make a fuss.*

Scrappy begins. "Prices aren't good, Arthur. You know that. Gettin' worse, too, and I don't believe we hit bottom yet."

"No. I don't neither."

"Pound of wool. I could get thirty-six cents for it a few years back. Down to fourteen now."

"That's a shame."

"You remember when we met in the store in town?"

"Yes, I do."

"What I liked about you was that you didn't want nothing on credit. You only bought what you had cash money for. I thought, *There's an honest young feller*. I glanced at your hands and could see you knew work, too. Hard work. It was right about then that I thought of hiring you, although I wanted to see you with your family, and I wanted Juanita's take on you too. Well, you know how it all worked out. Juanita and Mary took right to each other, just talkin' away."

"It worked out fine for us," says Arthur. "We are grateful to you and Juanita. And I hope it worked out fine on your end of the deal too."

"It has," says Scrappy, and he looks around again at the sky, the yet-fallow fields, the lazy smoke rising from the ditch. "But I did something I shouldn't have. Didn't follow my own rules. I bought some things on credit. Seemed like a good thing to do at the time, when prices were high and seemed to only be headed higher, and I was more ambitious than I should've been. Mistake though. I got sucked into it. I got played."

"Easy enough to do. The times seemed good. You're an optimist by nature anyway."

"So . . . me and the bank have become regular friends. I owe some, and it's a sure thing I ain't going to be getting it back at these prices. Corn. You can't hardly give it away, even for feed."

"I hear," Arthur says. Yes, of course he hears. The talk is everywhere—among the hired men, in town, at the store, and even over his own supper table, though he tries to steer away such conversation with his wife and children gathered around.

Scrappy stands a little taller and looks Arthur right in the eyes. He sets his mouth and spits out the next words, words that are hard for him, words he hoped he'd never have to say. "So I don't know if I can keep you on. Maybe. But I don't know. I'd rather do just about anything in this world than let you go or let you down. You know that you and Mary and the kids are family to me. But I don't know. I don't know how this is all going to play out, but I don't think it's going to come out good. And I can't keep you working if I can't pay you. That'd be wrong."

And Arthur thinks what a terrible thing it must be for Scrappy, gnarly fisted, sun beat, looking for the world as though he had a ton of weight and worry on his shoulders to tell him—a friend, not just a hired man—that there might not be enough. Scrappy looks weary and worn and, rare as it is, he takes off his hat and uses a bandana to wipe the sweat off the top of his head.

Arthur thinks, *Okay. Okay. I'll work something out.* Then he says, "So I'm done here?"

Scrappy says, "No. Not yet. I hope never. But I wanted you to know. After this, I got to go find Jim Deacon and let him go. But he's a youngster, no family to look after, so he can find a way to get by. Jim's a good boy, but I can't keep him on. Anyway, what I'm saying is, you might want to make some plans. Sorry."

And Arthur thinks, *I have my plan. I want to do what you've done. I want a quarter section to call my own, and I want to work it. But I guess that plan isn't going to be, at least for now.*

The conversation over, Scrappy scuttles back to his truck, solemnly nods in the general direction of Arthur, gets in, mouths the word "thanks" over the clatter of the engine, and drives slowly away.

And Arthur, he stands in the field there for a few moments, and he looks around at the land and sniffs the acrid smell of burned weeds, and it seems as though burning dreams come flaring at him and they seem to blow orange fire into his lungs and into his mind.

He doesn't want to think it, but he thinks it anyway, that Scrappy Burroughs looks like a tattered man on a stick. Arthur's world is tilting the wrong way on its axis, and he feels dizzy, and his vision gets narrow, narrow like he's seeing through a tube and everything just goes haywire for a minute. But he is Arthur Bell, and that is something. So what he says—because he says it aloud, is simple, and if you knew Arthur, it is the only thing he could say, even when he is worried and sick and feels more like lying down on the burned ground than anything else—is, "I won't tell Mary just yet. No need to worry her. She's got enough on her mind as is."

And he thinks, *I still have a little land, and that counts for something. I've got land. I am someone.* The land belongs to Arthur, but he also is wise enough to know that he belongs to the land. He thinks about Mary, he thinks of his sons, and his mouth curls into a grin when he thinks of Mercy May. *I've got land*, he thinks again. *And that counts too.*

And he climbs back down into the ditch and picks up the tossed-aside torch and strikes a match and goes back to work; he just goes back to work.

There are still weeds to burn.

Chapter Five

THEN THERE IS MERCY, JUST shy of nine years old, hazel-eyed, curly haired, with a smile that dazzles, short and sure and dancing through life like a water bug skimming across a drowsy July pond. She is the shooting star in the Bell family, tearing across a sky that grows slightly darker with each passing week. She is at the center of the family, joyful, fearless, sweet, and perceptive far beyond her years. She is a source of wonder to her brothers, a fountain of puzzlement and mystery to them. They cannot, for example, quite understand why she is suddenly reluctant to share the big upstairs bedroom with them, why she occasionally holds hushed conversations with Mary about needing privacy and a place to call her own, why she is given to occasional tears, why she no longer endures the farmyard teasing as she once did, and why she fusses so much with her hair when a simple part on the left side and maybe a clip is all she needed.

And they cannot fathom why she no longer plays as much second base on the family baseball team.

"Well, boys," says Arthur, looking into his four sons' eyes, searching for the right words, a search that often escapes many men. "She's a girl. That's what it is," he feebly explains one day as they work in the family garden plot, and Silas scrunches up his nose and makes a face and complains lightly about why Mercy May can get away with pouting about living with so many boys and needing a place to herself to be alone. The sons look at their father and wonder, a one-word question hanging unspoken in the air: "So?"

Arthur tries again. "Girls are different than boys. Girls need other things than boys, and one of 'em is they need their own places. And that's the way it is with your sister, and I understand it, and I hope you will too. That's just girls. Your mother and I have been talking a little about adding a room to the house. A room for your sister. Someday, you'll have a wife, and maybe you'll be a daddy to girls and you'll get it better then. But for now, that's about all I can tell you.

Girls are different, remember, but they're good to have around. Your mother is a girl, for example. Don't worry, we'll make do for a bit yet. I'm not going to put you all out in the barn to live. Not yet, anyway."

Arthur feels as though this part of his speech is reasonably articulate and reasonably accurate and his sons will reasonably understand and be reasonably content, for the most part. His sons, though, are more puzzled than ever and have just given up on it and figure someday things will make more sense, but in the meantime, they'll just have to hope that maybe they'll understand better sometime or their father will make things clearer and stammer less and not pull on his ear as much while doing so.

And it's just at that time that they hear the screen door slap hard against the frame, and Mercy May comes running out of the house full-bore, her knees pumping, her arms flying, her hair trailing behind her in a long ponytail that flops back and forth, back and forth, and to Arthur, it seems as though that ponytail is either waving hello to him or goodbye to him, and he really can't tell which, and maybe it's a case of both. But they all watch her with amazement and a little pride, and she is beloved by each of them, and for now, the talk about boys and girls and a new room for Mercy May and the potential for rebellion by the four Bell brothers is quelled just by the sight of their little sister running fast and carefree and unseen, or so she thinks.

And Arthur remembers a snippet of poetry as he sees her blasting forth in the morning sun from the house:

These became part of that child who went forth every day,
and who now goes, and will always go forth every day.

Arthur thinks the poem is by a fellow named Whitman, and he likes the poem because it talks about rearing children, and if he interprets it right, then Mr. Whitman was saying that almost everything that goes on about a child becomes a part of that child. And in the case of Mercy May, he thinks it means so many things are a part of her: Loving and kind parents, the land they all depend on, the magic of the soil, the crops, the animals, her brothers, the dark blue of a morning sky in the summer, the cold stars on a crackling December night, the fresh smell of turned earth, the sweet cool feeling that comes from walking through a frosty field in autumn. And Arthur thinks if his Mercy May is a part of all those things, from the family to the soil to the stars, if the poem writer Mr. Whitman has it right, then Mercy May is something, truly something.

And Arthur thinks he could never write poetry, but in this, Arthur is wrong again.

At school, Mercy May's penchant for poems helps her to step forward, helps distinguish her from the other girls who wear the same thready and frayed dresses to school each day, the little girls who attend just long enough to get the basics of reading and arithmetic and a few housekeeping skills and then disappear back to the farm to work and wait to be married and to bear children and then keep house for the rest of their lives until they turn listless and haggard, which happens all too soon.

But for Mercy May, it will be different. She knows it by the time she reaches the age of nine.

We turn here and begin a new part of Mercy May's life, the part about school.

She attends elementary school in a white-painted, two-room schoolhouse a little more than four miles from her home. It sits on the plain, the belfry standing higher than any other structure for some miles around, a wood-and-iron beacon of hope and promise on the dusty dry land. The school is divided down the middle by a thin wood wall, which chokes sound from one room to the other but does not cloak it. On one side, grades one through four gather and study; on the other, students in grades five through eight do similarly. To the side of the prim, neat schoolhouse is the teacher's house, constructed of the same pine planks as the school, barely three hundred square feet, plain as a shoebox, a window on the north side that allows the evening summer breeze to at least stir the air a bit, and a window on the south side so that the winter sunrays can stretch forth their radiant fingers and fetch away a bit of the chill from the house, which otherwise is warmed only by a clanky stove that burns coal and occasionally sagebrush.

Two classes, two teachers. They are Mr. and Mrs. Daniel P. Durham, late of western Pennsylvania, where they both went to and met at a teachers' college and, after having only known each other for a few months, married against the mild disapproving wishes of their families, both of which secretly held that each was marrying beneath the other, although time will prove with the solidity of basalt stone that both families were wrong in this matter.

Daniel Durham is of medium height, with dark hair parted to the left, and bespectacled, with a good face—a bit of an owlish face—a bushy handlebar mustache bedecking his upper lip, and a voice slightly higher than his appearance would indicate. Deep brown eyes; a ready smile; some training as a boxer; a fair intellect; and unabashed in his criticism of Mr. Herbert Hoover, a president whom he believes led the nation down a path from which it will not soon recover, and Daniel, in this belief, is right, as time is proving.

And then there is his wife, Anne, who is tall, of busty figure, hair always pulled in a tight dark-brown bun when in public, who walks purposefully, possessor of two strong hands and a wide back, and who seems as though she could be as at home in the lambing shed as she is in the classroom. She is not especially pretty, but one who could be and often is described as handsome, and she has the bearing of someone who sees more than is on the surface, who can assess character in an instant, and is infinitely patient. Anne Durham is well on her way to wisdom, though she doesn't yet know it, which is where all wisdom begins. She makes no pretense of her intellect; though actually brighter than her husband, she is content to allow him free range in his thought, conversation, and opinion.

She also bears no love for Mr. Hoover and holds great hope for Mr. Roosevelt.

Neither of them had ever been west of Cleveland when Daniel read a newspaper ad seeking the services of two teachers, preferably a married couple, to take on the task of sculpting the young and supple minds of the children of the Snake River Plain. The ad mentioned "challenge" and it mentioned "rewarding" and it mentioned "mountain views in every direction," which was a slight exaggeration; and it mentioned the "romantic West," which was a bald falsehood, but it was enough to get Daniel dreaming about life in a plush river valley filled with character and characters and a place where a man and his wife could breathe fresh mountain air and be inspired by the landscape and, someday, rear a brood of their own children far away from the suffocating ways of the East Coast. Heavens, maybe it was a place where he could write that book that had rattled around his head for so long. It all was a vision, clear, compelling, and beckoning.

So he and Anne talked and talked and thought hard about a new life in Idaho, and in the end, they answered the ad and sent a letter and were accepted as the new teachers at the small schoolhouse; them without seeing Idaho, and Idaho without seeing them.

Besides, they knew it was best to get away from their families who, for a time, would cause a quiet and steady grief if the couple elected to stay in Pennsylvania, as families sometime tend to do in newlywed matters. Moving west would teach their families a lesson, make their hearts ache for them, and prove that Daniel and Anne were entirely capable of making important decisions and acting in an independent and reasoned way.

They never will learn they were the only couple to apply, and it was only after they had been there some days that they recognized just how isolated they were from all conveniences and that the job opened up when the previous teacher, Mr. Halton J. Douglas, fell in love and eloped with Earlene Norbeck, who was his star pupil and, as it happened, an eighth grader, though seventeen years old. It was shortly after that the school board decided it was best to hire a married couple and perhaps avoid future shameful episodes that would cast a long and embarrassing shadow across the community and scrape away a layer of innocence from the students before their time.

The Durhams have no way of knowing in 1933 that they will live the rest of their lives on the plain and they will never have children because one of them can't, biologically speaking, and that Daniel will eventually become the school district superintendent and that Anne will become a trusted and beloved figure who will inspire hundreds of children to seek something better than the lives they know, and that she will indeed sculpt many young minds. And along the way, she will also learn how to be a first-rate midwife to bawling ewes ready to give birth, and the people on the plain will look at her as not only a handsome woman but a woman who can get things done, and it is the latter trait that earns her a special place in plain society.

And the Durhams do indeed prove to be hardworking, reasonable, and independent, and, in time, they are also right about making their families back East ache in their hearts because Idaho was so far away and Daniel and Anne might as well be colonizing a jungle in Panama as far as their parents are concerned.

Anne and Daniel take a train across the country and arrive in Twin Falls on a hot August afternoon. Daniel hires a wagon and has the driver from Warberg Transport take them to the schoolhouse and teacherage and, with soaring hopes and unbridled ambition, looks toward the Jarbidges and wonders which mountain glade would be theirs. Daniel fights back the faint little feeling that, from what he can see, the plains of southern Idaho don't appear to be all that scenic, are certainly not romantic, and that the fresh mountain air has the distinct odors of dung and dust. When the driver finally stops in front of the wood clapboard building and gruffly says, "Here's the school. There's the house. That'll be two dollars," the Durhams want to protest that this can't be the place; they want to take the wagon back to Twin, want to get on the next eastbound train and not get off until they are home in the East where they belong. The Warberg man looks at them sympathetically; they seem young and unsure, overwhelmed by the vast countryside, and horror-stricken by the small, plain, dodgy home they stand in front of. He thinks, *Two months. First time it gets cold, and they'll be back on the train for the East.* He repeats, "That'll be two dollars."

Anne gets off the wagon and sniffs the air and looks for the mountains, which seem so far away. Romantic West, bah. The wind blows hard, and little bits of sand and soil and grit glance off her face and she has to hold on to her frilly eastern hat, and when the driver drops their bags and trunk on the side and drives off, she looks at Daniel and says, "Where are the mountains?"

And he looks puzzled and says, "I am unsure," and though a strong woman, Anne bursts into tears. Had she looked a little more to the southwest, and if the air was not so thick with summer haze, she would have seen the Jarbidges shimmering in the evening heat, and had she looked far to the north, she might have seen the Centennials and Pioneers jutting skyward, and maybe she would have felt a little better; but really, she can't take in more than the disappointing schoolhouse, the small teacher's home, and the Mormon crickets, which are at this time climbing up her dress and into her sleeves and hair; and she can only think one oppressive thought that circles around and around inside her head like a big spokey wheel on a hard-pedaling bicycle: *What have we done? What have we done? What have we done?*

It is finally Daniel who takes a deep breath, calmly picks up a trunk, and says, "They told us in the letter that the teacherage would be unlocked. We'd better go in and see what we can make of this place. It isn't much, is it, dear?" And he looks around again at the dry, golden plain, the faraway velvety mountains dancing in the early evening heat, and feels his heart move, though just a little.

And with that, Anne grimly nods and picks up a small suitcase, and years later, she will tell people she believed at that point that she was walking to certain despair and desolation, if not possible death; that she, for an instant, questioned not only the judgment of her husband but also her love for him; and that she concentrated only on one thought: how could she get away from this forsaken place, and how soon?

But they find a bed, and they find some bedding that a kind soul from the school board had left, and late that night, when the sky clears and the custard moon floods the small house with pale-yellow light and a coyote wails and the air becomes soft and a cool breeze comes calling from the slopes of the Jarbidges; late that night, when she lay close to Daniel in a thin cotton nightgown and he strokes her hair and pulls her even closer; and after she puts her head on his chest and he murmurs to her, "It will be all right, it will be all right"; and in the morning, when the sun creeps over the ridge to the east and a robin trills and a meadowlark whistles its three-note call, and a tardy night owl whooshes its wings on its way to a daytime perch; a tiny bit of peace settles in her and takes root in her heart. A godsent calm washes over her, and as the rays chase away the black, the purple, and the gold, and usher in a marble-blue sky, she thinks the least she can do is see the place in the justice of the full light of day.

And she looks at the sun as it is rising and thinks, *I have never seen the sun look that big*, and that big-old sun is like a promise or maybe an answer to a prayer, and she thinks she can smell the sky and it smells moist, even though it will be another month before a drop of rain falls. All of it confuses her, and yet, being confused makes her feel very much alive, and it is at that moment she learns that sometimes you have to trade safety and security and what passes for normal in exchange for bewilderment and fright to really feel life swarming about you, with you in the smack-dab middle of it, trying to take it all in and figure it all out.

And feeling alive is exactly when something begins to turn in her and her views about the southern Idaho Plain.

She quietly slides from bed, finds her shoes, and takes off on a walk. She goes to the west and then a little to the north. She sees the fields, copper brown in late summer, and little houses sticking up off the plain like dark stone raisins on a sheet of light wheat bread, and she wonders if any children she might teach live in them. Then she finds a little stream that tumbles down from the Jarbidge Mountains, and she takes off her shoes and nestles under a willow tree and just listens; she only listens. Finally, she falls asleep, the gurgling of the water, the whish and whoosh of the wind, the hum of more morning songbirds, all combining to a lullaby that overpowers her in a slumbery ease.

How long she sleeps she cannot tell, but the sun is higher in the sky and doesn't seem quite so large, and her face and neck are warm. She gets up quickly and retraces her path back to the teacherage, thinking hard the whole way. She sees Daniel in front of the house, worry lines spider-webbing across his forehead; pacing, hands in pockets, dressed in his proper eastern traveling pants, barefoot, a white ribbed undershirt flapping over the top of his trousers. He looks up and sees her, and the worry lines almost go away.

"Anne! Anne! I thought you had left for home! I am so sorry to have brought you all this way here. We can write a letter of resignation and drop it off at the school board chairman's house in town and be back in Pennsylvania in a week's time." And he holds out his hands for her, and his hands shake. "Perhaps it's where we belong. This country is too hard for us."

And she smiles and says, "But dear Daniel, we *are* at home. I believe I'd like to stay and try this. Our contract is for a year, so a year is what we will stay." She glances around her, at the dry land, the powdery road, the small, dilapidated house, the rundown school, and calls upon her stores of courage. "This place is not without its charms."

He cannot believe what he said. Joy surges through his body, and he walks briskly toward his wife. It is exactly what he had hoped to hear but never thought he would. And because he loves Anne, he would have pretended to dislike this place of grit and wind as much as she did and lead her back east. Daniel, you see, had fallen in love with the dry, rough plain by sundown the first night.

And now Anne too had become a sudden and unexpected convert. For a year, at least.

They walk back to the thumb-sized house, arm-in-arm, and Anne begins to sweep it out and think about hanging curtains, and Daniel climbs on the roof to look for places where it might need patching, and it is there that he notices those tall, slate-blue mountains to the north—what he believes are the Centennial Mountains—shimmering, it seems, in the air, just above the plain.

He gulps in the sight of those mountains, and his breath draws in with a pang, a good pang, the kind that comes as a swift, sure sign of a decent surprise. The sight of those mountain peaks, he believes, is a sign of tall futures, a sign of big vision, a sign of hope in days to come.

***

Less than two weeks later, the first day of school, and Anne Durham stands at the front of her classroom and watches the children—first, second, third, and fourth graders—scuff their way into the classroom, settle nervously in their chairs, and stare at her, eyes big and wide and round, questions inching into their minds like spiders under a doorsill about the new teacher, the poignant and popular one being, *Will she be nice?*

They cannot tell by a glance. She is tall and wears a long gray skirt and a white cotton blouse with billowy sleeves and a little red ribbon that hangs down across her breasts. Her face tells them little. It is neither friendly nor unfriendly, although an occasional slight nod and smile and swift, "Good morning," are parceled out as students enter and curiously look her way.

They have heard that the new teacher for the lower grades would be a woman and that her husband would teach the upper grades. It is a curious arrangement, they think; a man and his wife working side by side, living in the house only a stone's throw away from the school. They wonder what happened to Mr. Douglas, although the older students in the other half of the schoolhouse all seem to know. They'd heard too much of muted conversations at home, the mumbling that the short, foolish, imperious Mr. Douglas had better get out or be thrown out, and the sooner the better for all parties concerned. And none of them had seen Earlene since late May.

In front of the room, Anne feels the pull of many currents and thinks, *My. Oh. Dear. What shall I say to them? What can I possibly teach them?* And she thinks more, *Is there a student of promise among them? A future doctor or nurse or teacher? Is there any good I can do here? What am I doing here?* And the faces just stare at her. She stares back. She wonders if her clothing makes her too schoolmarmish in appearance.

And in the silent, strong standoff, she looks at her students, and they look at her and wonder, *What can she teach us?*

But is she nice?

Anne gives off little in the way of clues because she is almost rigid with worry and fright. She feels herself perspiring and wonders if it is the early morning dry heat or her nerves or if she is not feeling well and concludes it is probably part of each. *You are in Idaho. Idaho! For heaven's sake. What are you doing here?* she thinks, and the doubts come swooshing in all again. She has a plan for the first day before her, written in her tall, straight hand, but it may as well be in hieroglyphics; the letters and words all seem to shake and shimmy and slide together into an undecipherable jumble. All her will is concentrated on merely standing at the front of the classroom, the perfunctory greeting, and not passing out. She has one primitive question, as well: *Will they be nice boys and girls?*

And then she notices a little sprite of a girl—second-grader, she judges; curly, dark-brown hair; plain white dress; shoes that look too big for her; shy, beguiling smile; and a red apple in her left hand. Mercy May sees the new teacher staring at her; their gazes lock, and Mercy May, used to teasing from four older brothers and, by the same token, used to holding her own ground against the taunts of four older brothers, makes a long, oval face at her teacher and sticks out her tongue. And then, registering the surprise on the face of Anne and taking it as a sign of winning the skirmish with this tall, formal, and formidable schoolteacher, Mercy May gives her an over-the-top, dramatic wink of her left eye.

Boundaries established, the little girl then stands up and marches to the teacher's desk and hands her the apple.

"For you, Teacher. My mother said I should give it to you."

Anne regains part of her composure and says, "Thank you. I love apples." And then, thinking, *This is Idaho and not western Pennsylvania, and some things are different here, and you need, Anne Durham, to adjust as the occasion calls for*, she sticks out her tongue at Mercy May and gives her an exaggerated wink. "I see we have a few things in common," she says. "I hope this is the beginning of many discoveries." And she asks the small girl with pawing feet in front of her, "What is your name?"

And the small girl replies, "My name is Mercy May. Mercy May Bell. When my mother had me, she said, 'Mercy!' and that's how I got my name. I don't think it's easy having a baby. I've seen pig sows do it. Sheep ewes too. It's messy and looks hard."

The teacher smiles again and tries in vain to stifle a small, delicate laugh, which floats throughout the room. It is far different from the crisp, cadenced "Good morning" the students had heard to that point, and the same thought occurs among every young girl and boy in the room, the phrase that they will repeat when their parents ask them about the new teacher at supper that night: *The teacher seems nice. We heard her laugh. She's tall. She doesn't talk like we do. And she stuck her tongue out at Mercy May Bell.*

But for that moment, Anne feels a flood of gratitude for the little girl and her kind gesture, as well as for the silly face she made and the big, sassy wink, and she says, "Thank you, Mercy May Bell. I think we shall become friends."

And in this statement, time proves Anne Durham to be much more than a teacher. In this statement, directed to a poppy seed of a young girl, she proves to be a prophetess.

Chapter Six

Scrappy Burroughs sits at the oak supper table in his home and looks at four letters, all typed, all official, all foreboding, all telling him the stark truth of what he is about to lose. He shuffles them, first one on top, then another, the second letter dropping to third, the third shoved to the bottom of the pile. He shuffles them as if he hopes their message will somehow change if he mixes them up and reads them in another order, but their message remains the same. He spreads them with his large knuckled fingers and peers at them again with gray eyes sheltered by a thicket of salt-and-pepper eyebrows. He is dressed in his overalls and a soiled brown shirt, his faded, grubby felt fedora pulled tight to his floppy ears. Scrappy Burroughs has a good face—not handsome but full of character and a worn wisdom etched in every wrinkle, every brown splotch calved by too many days under a harsh sun.

It is the letter from the sheriff dated October 29, 1933, that bothers him most. He has known Sheriff Forrest Prater before the lawman even knew he would become a lawman. Voted for him three times. He is a man whom Scrappy Burroughs likes and respects, and he wonders how painful it must have been for Forrest Prater to sign the letter, how much he must have dreaded the act of taking pen to paper and scribbling his name.

He thinks some more, and the same words bubble up, words that seem to have carved ruts in his mind: *Crops in, not a good harvest, too dry. Prices low and dropping lower, fast. Spuds. Couldn't get a dollar for a full gunny bag. Bills. Bills to pay and nothing to pay them with.*

Shouldn't have borrowed for the Farmall tractor a few years back, but it seemed as though it'd pay for itself in almost no time. That shiny red tractor. Could do about anything with it, and oh, how he loved to sit on top and drive it. He wishes he could pay it off, along with every other bill. But with what? How? How can this all work?

And now it looks as though there will be a sheriff's auction two days before Christmas. Everything Scrappy owns will be on the block, everything short of his house and land, and he wonders if they'll have to be sold too, just to pay the bills. But he *will* pay them. Scrappy Burroughs never has taken anything that he didn't earn, pay for, or acquire in an honest swap, and he isn't going to start backing out of anything now at age fifty-four. He thinks, *I may not leave much behind, but I will take a good name to the grave and not owe any man.*

He has six people on the payroll. All steady men, all hard workers. Of the six, it was Arthur Bell that panged him most. More like a younger brother to him, hardest worker of all. And his kids. Four boys and that little bug of a girl. How could he even think of letting Arthur go? Well, he couldn't. Just couldn't. He'd find a way somehow. He'd spoken to the men about work and what they might expect, and not a one seemed surprised, not a flinch or wince among them. *They know what's going on,* he thinks, *how bedraggled the world seems to be, how the hope in a man can fray from a thick corded rope to a strand of thread in almost no time.*

But, he figures, *at least we got that strand to hang on to. And for now, it will have to do.*

Scrappy Burroughs sighs and surmises that it's going to be some Christmas, what with no goods, no money, and precious little holiday joy. He stands up from the table and folds the letters and puts them deep in a pocket of his overalls. He shuffles to the front door. A little breeze shushes through the screen door, chilling him.

Like other farmers and ranchers gritting through hard times, he looks to the land for his hope. If you've got land, you've got hope. It's that simple. He pushes through the doorway and sits in a wood chair on the porch and soaks in the sounds of nightfall. Those sounds soothe him, help his taut muscles to unwind and, for a moment, forget about the four letters in his pocket, and in his mind, he starts lining out the morning chores.

***

This is the October no rain will fall, although crop prices will. Sometimes big, billowy clouds take shape to the south, over the mountains in the hot afternoons, and the men look up with hope and think those blue-black nimbus clouds will blow their way and drop rain upon a parched land. The men wet their fingers and check which way the wind is blowing and calculate the probable path of the thunderstorms, but the thunderstorms seem to pale and weaken and die before getting to the Snake River Plain, and all that is left is a dry wind, a faraway virga, another layer of grit, the clatter of blowing wind, and rows of dried-out crops.

The canals help, but it has to rain and snow to keep a canal full. Good rain makes good farmers, they all know.

And October will stretch into November and November into December and hardly a drop will fall. The moon comes up on harvest nights, looking more brown than golden, and the sun rises plum red each morning because of the smoke and dust in the air.

Snow. There should be snow in the mountains by now—at least a frosting's worth—but no. Nothing. And every farmer knows snow in the fall is the first sign of a decent water year ahead. Early snow is hope, but there is no snow and no hope.

The land and crops dry, prices continue their dizzying descent, and a quick and cruel Nature entwines them all in a joint dusty destiny.

And families begin to wither too.

Anne Durham notices it soon after the school year starts. A boy, a girl, brother and sister, sit big-eyed in class one day and then the next, but by Wednesday of the week, they're gone. The absence of one, maybe that is illness, of which there seems to be plenty on the plain; two gone together without a word, and that meant the family likely packed up and slipped away without a word spoken to friends or neighbors, not to mention the eastern-bred schoolteachers.

"Can anyone tell me," she asks the classroom, knowing beforehand the answer she would get, "what happened to the Archer children? Paul and Bonnie Jean?"

And the children shuffle their feet and look down and maybe shoot a glance out the one window on the side of the schoolhouse, and there might be a titter at the back of the room, the older students in scritchy voices saying, "She don't know, does she? She don't know that Paul and Bonnie Jean moved out last night. Paul told me on the way home yesterday."

Finally, one of the children shyly raises a hand and says, "They're gone. They moved. They was going to try things in Oregon."

And that's the way it is. Families pack up what they can, leave behind much of what they had, and move to where the father might be able to find a job. California is where most of them head, where there are work camps and the drought is not near so bad and the harvests are still decent and the picking season is long. The weather is so mild you could toss a tarp over a tree branch and be warm and fine. And tales of oranges and apples and grapes, weighing down so heavy that the branches just snap. "You can feed your family off what falls from those trees and vines," some people say. Never go hungry, not at all, and the rain comes regularly and there's work, always work, and if you need a few months just to get back on your feet and not have the dust caking your face and get down inside your clothes and throat, that's where you should go, to California. "What I'd give," they'd say, "for an orange right off the tree, sweet and juicy."

So many go to California, and none of them, not a one, ever make their way back to the Idaho Plain, and most are never heard of again. Gone. They just vanish, and their lives in Idaho blow away in front of the hot, gritty wind, like the blue-black clouds that form with promise in the afternoon and then peter out before a drop can fall on the plain.

Not all go to California though. Some go to Oregon and Washington, to lumber camps. Others, the most fortunate, find jobs with the railroad. But most find no steady work at all, and they drift and, with them, their children drift too, settling in a place like flimsy butterflies on a flower, there only long enough for the next puff of hot, dry air to move them along again.

In the beginning, it bothers Anne, and Daniel too. They get attached to those kids, help them read a little better, get their numbers down cold, maybe even light a quick little flame in their minds. And then the children are gone, and the two schoolteachers sometimes lie awake at night and ask, "Do you wonder what became of the Archer kids? I wonder about Raymond Carter and his sister, Nora. Bright kids, both of them. They had potential. I wonder if they'll make it; probably no, the odds are against them. Hope they're eating regularly."

But after a while, after so many of the children move almost in the middle of the night, the Durhams begin to understand and grudgingly accept it. Part of life in southern Idaho. Part of their fathers and mothers not being able to put down roots. Part of not having any money, part of not having any future. Part of being hungry, part of being desperate to take care of your family. In the end, Anne and Daniel come to accept that their stewardship over these children is most likely temporary, and the best they can do is prepare the vagabonds for the next small schoolhouse they'd attend and hope that a teacher there would take up where they left off, and if the children were most fortunate, that a teacher might feel for them and their plight and might even love them. And with despair, Anne sometimes thought that even if she were fortunate enough to find a student of promise, the student simply may not show up someday—gone, moved on, fled, as if a howling blizzard had swept them away.

The schoolteachers are not alone in mourning those who lose everything or might lose everything.

But Juanita Burroughs will not let her family wither away. She stands in her kitchen and pours water into a bucket and scrubs the supper dishes. She is a stout, strong woman of fifty years, mostly silver haired, matronly, droop shouldered from seasons of hard work and bearing babies, quick and efficient in her movement.

She's seen two dozen families pack and leave, some of them all in a night—gone, vanished, blown away like dust beams on a windowsill by a puff of hot, dry wind. No one has a bigger heart, a kindlier disposition, or more charitable ways. And no one has more steel and strength in her fiber. She talks to Scrappy as he sips coffee in the evening twilight, pencil in hand, jotting figures, gazing over yet another small mound of letters, trying to spin a bit of magic and somehow make everything all work out.

"Makin' any progress, Scrappy?"

He fidgets and his pencil flies over brown paper and he says, "Nope. Nothing."

"When's the sale scheduled?"

"Couple of days before Christmas. Makes you wonder if the bank people have hearts. My guess is no."

"We'll be fine at Christmas," she says, although she speaks with more confidence than she feels. "We'll be together at least." And then, to change the subject, "How are prices?"

"Down and getting downer."

"Am I bothering you?"

"A little, just a little, Juanita."

And for long minutes she only hears the scratching of soft graphite on the crinkly brown paper, an occasional slurp, the creak from the chair as Scrappy, a big man, shifts from side to side. She cannot remain silent. She says, "So what are we going to do, honey? Give it up and move on?"

And he puts his pencil down and raises his eyes to the ceiling, and since he is a man who doesn't want to groan—strong men do not groan in front of their families—he just sighs, then he grunts, and he feels as though his heart and head are going to burst, and he says, "I don't know just yet, but I can't move from here. It's where we belong. It's the land. I don't know if I own it or it owns me. Maybe I can talk to the bank. Might be worth a try."

And Juanita, though she knows better, cannot refrain from asking the heavy, prickly question, "What about Arthur? Can you at least keep him on until Christmas?"

And Scrappy says, "I don't think so."

And Juanita knows the thought of turning Arthur loose is harder on her husband than the thought of having his own family someday closing the door of their own empty home, putting the key under the doormat, and slowly turning away for the final time.

Scrappy Burroughs cannot bear the thought of letting down a friend.

***

So Scrappy, two days later, dresses up in his finest and goes into town to talk with Mr. Edgar Neely, the bank's vice president. Scrappy knows well the name Neely; an old boy a dozen miles to the east, good farmer, died a few years ago while digging out potatoes, just plopped over fifty feet from his house. Bang. Heart attack.

Scrappy thinks, *Maybe if the bank Neely understands I knew his father, maybe things will go easier.* It was time he wanted, not more money, just time. Not that he expected any undue help, but maybe young Neely would look more charitably on a friend of his father's. A man needs a break, needs something to bend his way. It sure wasn't coming from the sky or the seeds he planted, not from the crop prices that were dropping like fat, cold hailstones, but maybe it would come from Neely at the bank.

Scrappy gets in the old pickup, dressed in a worn white shirt, denim pants, and an old blue tie strapped around his collar, which he thinks feels about the same as a noose. He dusts off the ancient fedora and reshapes it a bit, the least little the oily hat will stand for, and starts the truck. One of his field hands calls out to him, "Hey, who died, boss? You're decked out like you was going to a funeral."

On the Snake River Plain, men such as Scrappy Burroughs only wear a tie to funerals and weddings, and this being Tuesday morning, there are no weddings; *and no one has died,* he thinks, *at least nobody yet.* Scrappy Burroughs conjures a smile and cheerfully calls back, "Just goin' to town, a little business to take care of. Nobody's dead that I know of."

He puts the truck in gear and rumbles down the road and sends up big spraying clouds of dust behind him. The early November sun has made the cab unseasonably hot even with the windows down. He begins to sweat from heat and nerves, and the clean, pressed shirt soon feels soiled and limp, and he understands he is not at his best.

He makes his way to town and pulls in front of the stone bank with its Greek columns and parks at an angle, the nose of the old truck pointed downward toward the useless gutter.

He gets out of the truck and takes a quick look at himself in the reflection of a window. *Well, Mr. Banker,* he thinks, *this is who I am and what you get today—Scrappy Burroughs—nothing more, nothing less*; and he loosens the coarse wool tie and walks in.

A line of young male tellers with dark, oily hair parted down the middle stand behind a tall, polished wood counter. Scrappy tries not to think how much they resemble a gaggle of vultures. To the side of them in the large gray room, a plump bespectacled woman fiddles with a typewriter, adjusting a piece of yellow carbon paper behind the roller, and it is she whom Scrappy Burroughs approaches. "I'm here to see Edgar Neely. The name is Burroughs," and he's bothered by the tightness in his throat, which he blames on the accursed necktie.

She looks up at him, and he's relieved when she smiles and says, "I'll let him know you're here," and she rises from her desk, and her shoes make a clop-clop-clop sound, and her skirt and stockings make a swish-swish-swish sound, and she disappears around the corner for a moment then reappears and says, "He's this way." And with a beckon of her head and a hand stretched forth to point the way, Scrappy Burroughs is directed to a quieter part of the bank.

Edgar Neely is youngish, in his mid-thirties, fair skinned, sharp nosed, small eyed, and has wispy hair somewhere between brown and copper, and a thin mustache that seems to be struggling to take root in his upper lip. Scrappy Burroughs tamps down his impulse to make quick judgment, although it is a trait that has served him well in most ways. Still, he cannot help thinking that Edgar Neely looks a bit like a magpie but with less character in his face.

"Good morning, Mr. Burroughs."

"Mornin' to you, Mr. Neely." And Scrappy Burroughs takes off his hat and holds it in his hands, grasps it with twitchy fingers, and wishes he hadn't worn it at all.

"What can I do for you?" Edgar Neely says with thick, artificial pleasantness.

Scrappy looks around because what he is about to say is private and he doesn't want anyone to hear it and it reminds him of the last time he went to a doctor, back in 1922, when he had a deep, craggy cough that wracked his chest in pain, a cough that wouldn't go away for months and the bulgy-eyed doctor had said, "Can you take off your shirt, Mr. Burroughs, and let me listen to your lungs?" and Scrappy had said fiercely, no, he would not take off his shirt and anything his lungs had to say to the doctor he could darn well hear through it.

"Well, Mr. Neely, it's like this. I got some debt, as you know, and I ain't sure how I'll pay it off, but I will. All's I really need is more time, and help from Mother Nature, and it's bound to rain sometime because droughts don't last forever, and the prices, well, them prices have got to come up too. They can't stay in the cellar forever."

Scrappy pauses for breath and is startled to hear the sound of his thudding heart. "I am good on my word and when I say to you that I will pay every cent I owe, plus interest, you can"—and Scrappy thinks he shouldn't say, "take it to the bank," so he says,—"count on me because I never got nothing in my life without paying for it. And I can't make it rain or raise crop prices and neither can you, but your bank can give me time. I don't want to lose everything, and I want to keep my things because they will help get me out of this hole. Like my tractor and animals and disc and such. I'm sorry I borrowed so much."

It is the longest oration of Scrappy Burroughs's entire life. He is exhausted, and he would give almost anything to be back home, doing chores, joking and laughing with the hired men.

The reedy little banker listens impassively and then pulls a file from his desk drawer, and Scrappy can see, to his horror, that his name is on it and in it are copies of all the letters that he has seen and read and stewed and fretted over, those letters that kept him awake at night and made his stomach feel more like an oil-less gear box in his tractor than something to aid in the digestion of his daily bread earned by the sweat of his brow just as was the way with the man Adam.

Mr. Neely looks through the file, and his eyes dart from paper to paper, and he makes a little humming sound from time to time, and his pink fingers fly across the paper, and he has a rubber thumb cap on that helps him rapidly sort through the sheaf. Mr. Neely daintily clears his throat and says, "Mr. Burroughs. You're in a very bad way. My duty is to protect the assets of the bank, and as much as I'd like to help you, you leave me little choice. Everything will proceed as has been repeatedly outlined to you in the letters."

Scrappy Burroughs raises a hand in protest, but the banker drones on. "Your house may be in jeopardy at some future point. The law is with us. Good day, Mr. Burroughs."

"But ain't I part of your bank, and ain't I part of the investment?" Scrappy is surprised at his thunderous blurt and surprised even more by the feeling that he has just been socked in the gut. "Can't you believe in *me*?"

Mr. Edgar Neely puts aside his file and says earnestly, "What I believe in are numbers. They tell the truth. Not you, not your emotional outbursts. You are, I repeat, in a dire situation. All creditors must be satisfied to the degree possible."

And Scrappy Burroughs feels as though he has been accused of telling a lie because his intentions have been honorable and noble his entire life. Something inside him fizzes and hisses and explodes like a Roman candle, and a dark, fierce anger boils to the surface.

"You!" he shouts. "You! You don't know the land! I helped carry your daddy out of the church in his casket. We got roots together! You make a livin' by sittin' at a desk and acting prissy and looking at your numbers and telling people 'no'! You never knew the feel of a good harvest or worrying about rain or thinking at night about crickets eating your crops! Somewheres you forgot about being human. We count for more than what you got on your infernal ledger! You! You! You!"

And that becomes the second-longest speech Scrappy has ever uttered.

Scrappy Burroughs regrets that at a moment when a ripe, scarlet curse aimed at Mr. Edgar Neely would have been much more personally satisfying, the only invective he could muster was "You!" For this he feels ashamed, but he should not because the one word, bellowed in rage, did just fine; it laid all the frustration and disappointment and heartache right at the feet of the smug young man behind the desk.

Still, Scrappy Burroughs wonders if one good ripened word woven into pointed and eloquent phrasing, aimed with precision, timed just right, spoken slowly and with menace, would have struck home true. He is sure the answer to the question is yes.

And young Mr. Edgar Neely smiles placidly and slightly motions his head, and a bank guard saunters toward Scrappy Burroughs. Edgar Neely has been confronted by angry farmers before. He knows how to handle them, and the way to handle them is to nod slightly to the bulky guard and have the angry farmer removed from the bank.

Beads of sweat break from Scrappy Burroughs's forehead and on his arms and under his sleeves, and his heart pounds and his tongue feels thick, but he's not quite done with all he wants to say. A furious and righteous loquaciousness has descended upon him. "Your daddy was a good man and a good farmer. You're nothing like him. He'd be ashamed of what you've become, Edgar Neely."

He feels the guard's hand on his shoulder. He stands up and says, "I'm leaving. I don't want to stay in this stinking place any longer than I have to." He takes a step and then announces to all within earshot shrilly, sarcastically, "And a Merry Christmas to you and your all."

He looks over his shoulder once more with a venomous glance at Mr. Edgar Neely, who calmly shuffles papers on his desk and avoids making eye contact.

The bank is quiet, and the tellers follow the heavy, thudding movement of Scrappy Burroughs until he pushes through the big oak double doors. *Another one*, they think.

The plump young woman at the desk looks at him with pity and thinks what she does for a living isn't much of a job. *It pays, and I'm inside a building, out of the heat and dust and cold*, she reminds herself. *And I don't top sugar beets or pull spuds out of the ground, but I've seen too many broken men go through those doors, and I don't like it, and I wonder how much longer I can take it.* She pushes her wire glasses lower on her nose, bows her head, and resumes typing.

The road home for Scrappy Burroughs is bumpy and blurry, and he drives as if in a trance. He slinks through the doorway. Juanita raises her head, and the question asked is unspoken; not a word is exchanged, yet they both understand. And Scrappy Burroughs looks glum, and the punchy feeling in his stomach is as strong as ever, and his shoulders sag and his arms are loose at his sides, and then he lifts his hands and takes off the wretched tie and flings it across the room and pushes the ancient fedora off his head and lets it drop to the floor and says, "I don't think I done us any good today."

Chapter Seven

BACK FROM LUNCH AT THE resort's dining room, she reads, though it is difficult for her, then rests. The sun dodges among the clouds, blinking and sending down shafts of sunlight here and there. The earth is moist and rich, as it always seems to be in western Oregon. Old-growth Douglas firs tower to the south of her room, beyond her roses, beyond the green grassy slope just outside her window. My mother stretches and then speaks in a soft, crinkly voice. Tonight, the words are mostly coming easily, almost as if the stroke had not occurred.

"Mr. Burroughs saved us. He was so good to us. And Mr. Bowker, too. What an intriguing and . . . sad man he was. The Andrews twins. Such fun, and good men too. Every girl on the plain had . . . a crush on one of them or . . . both of them. And Mrs. Durham. Do you know, I'd never been to a . . . you know, oh, the place with books . . . a library until she took me there one Saturday? It came as such a surprise. I had passed by the library . . . many times and thought it was for wealthy people. Mother told me that. What a heavenly spot it became to me."

She puts her book down and begins to doze. On cue, the sun hides behind clouds and shadows envelope her room. She starts for a moment, strains at words to describe her memories, and then the words tumble out.

"Heroes," she says. "They were all heroes, and my father too. Hard times make heroes of common people."

And she quietly falls asleep.

***

Early December, chilly, high, pearly cirrus clouds in the sky, snow only at the tops of the mountains to the north and east. Mary Bell is on her small back porch, two oval tubs perched on an old barn plank, stretched across two blocks of wood. She pours in heated water. She slices a small bar of soap and drops the shavings into one of the tubs where the soap bobs and wiggles, quickly bringing it to a frothy, foamy head. The steam rises in clouds and whirls, and she reaches for a pair of boy's overalls and plunges them into the hot, soapy water. She scrapes the overalls against the scrubby washboard and counts a rhythm in her head: swoosh up, swoosh down, swoosh up, swoosh down, pound and turn, pound and turn.

Squeeze against the side, twist, and squeeze some more. Dip into the rinse tub, swirl around, squeeze against the side, crank the cloth through her small hand wringer, hang them to dry on the thin cord tied between a corner of the house and a stout Russian olive tree.

One garment done. Maybe thirty more wait in the pile of dirty clothes.

Her hands are red and wrinkly. Big half-moon circles droop below her eyes. Her back muscles spasm, white-hot pain flashes through her arms and shoulders. Washing clothes by hand for a family of seven is a day-long job with only time for preparing meals and a bit of idle chit-chat with the children. She would never say so, but she dreads Tuesday, washing day. In winter, the work of laundry is even more toilsome because it is cold and the wind bellows across the plain and the clothes still must be hung on the line and freeze-dried.

She is thirty-six years old, feels like sixty, and when Arthur speaks to her quietly in the night and they talk about adding another child, maybe a boy, one more boy to do chores for the time when Arthur's body begins to give way, to help carry them into their old age, she thinks of how tired she feels, the sheer exhaustion of her days, and she muses, "There will be no old age for me. This is what it must feel like; I know it already," and she turns away from her gentle husband because she can't bear the thought of another little one to care for, bringing another baby into a world that seems to grow only harder and make less sense every day.

She is lost in thought, just she and the laundry and her aching wrists and her raw, rheumy hands, and she finishes another pair of overalls and squeezes them through the wringer. Arthur walks into the house and then to the back porch, where he sees her bent over, squeezing a denim work shirt through the wringer. He is home even though the sun still sits high and is far from saddling behind the low hills to the west.

She sees him and knows something is not right because Scrappy Burroughs does not send men home early.

"Dear?" she says.

The one word is an invitation for him to speak, and it is fraught with anxiety. She looks at him in his dirty clothes and the dust hanging on top of his head so thick it almost seems his hair is more blond than brown, and she fears that something is about to get worse, and she wonders if the next piece of news will break her.

Arthur stoops in the dirt just off the porch and makes a big circle in the soil with his index finger. "I'm home," is all he can think to say.

"Something wrong?" she asks.

"Scrappy. What he told us today. He says he can't afford to pay us no more, and he says that if he can't pay, he can't ask us to work. So he told us to go home." And there, in the backyard, in the dirt, squatting on the balls of his feet, he writes something in the soil, but Mary cannot read it from where she is.

Face down, Arthur scribbles some more. "How much we got saved?"

Mary, the family banker, hesitates and rolls her eyes skyward and says, "We have twenty-something dollars in the sugar bowl. I have three dollars in my top drawer. I have a bit of change in the Mason jar over the stove. Not much. Maybe a couple dollars more."

Arthur nods, still kneeling, and speaks sheepishly. "And I have four, maybe five dollars in a place I never told you about."

Mary says, "So that's enough for a month, maybe six weeks, if we're careful. Two months if we count pennies."

And Arthur says, "The garden came in good. I could shoot a few birds yet this fall."

Then, an uncomfortable silence. He says nothing. Mary says nothing. A minute, then two, then five, and ten slide by without a word, a deafening silent thunder.

"What else are we going to do?" Mary finally asks.

Arthur says, "I don't know. We'll figure out something. We've always managed."

And Mary says, "But it seems different this time. We can't move again, Arthur. We've got a little place, this old stone house. And what if we move and there's no work where we go? Then what? And where? Montana, to a silver mine? Picking in California? Lumbering in Oregon?"

She looks at him, wishes he would look up at her, but he just traces something more in the dirt. Then she answers her own question. "Running again, that's where. I'm tired of running, Arthur. I am so very tired."

She wrings through another shirt and pins it to the line.

Four down. Twenty-six more.

"I know. I think we need to sit tight here. Just seems smarter."

"Yes," she says. "Yes."

"Won't be much of a Christmas," Arthur says.

"It's okay. Gifts at Christmas don't count for much anyway."

Mary turns to Arthur and squats beside him. Arthur is still on his haunches, slowly tracing in the dirt. She sees in him a man almost beat, a man who does not know what to do other than write curious words and numbers in the soil of the yard, words and figures that will soon enough blow away.

"Does Scrappy still have work to do?"

"Plenty."

Arthur looks up, feeling the gaze of his wife. "He's been good to us," she says.

"I know," he says, rising from the ground. "I know he has, but . . ." and his eyes wander to the sky, and he sees a big crow flying and hears it caw, and it seems to be poking fun at these forlorn and hopeless humans on the ground, and for a breath, Arthur wishes he were up there in the air with the big black crow and no earthly cares. "I'll be home 'round supper."

And with that, he jams his hands into his pockets, his head tilting downward, and moves around to the side of the house and begins to walk across the land, out toward the road.

***

Scrappy Burroughs is pulling the last of the sugar beets from the ground. He expertly digs them up, tops them, and drops them into the gunny bag he pulls along with him. The work is arduous and painful. His back is sore, particularly down on the left side, pinching hard the same place every time he stoops for another beet and every time he tries to stand up straight.

Price of sugar beets. Couldn't get a quarter for the entire bag. Forget about breaking even. He digs another beet and grimaces when the curly ribbon of pain stabs him.

He hears feet shuffling through the field, the familiar soft sound of boots and denim brushing against sugar beets. *Maybe it's Juanita,* he thinks without glancing up. A shadow falls on him, the shadow of a man, medium height, sinewy build. Then he hears a voice, and it is not the voice of his wife, yet it is a voice of tender hope.

"You intend to clean this whole field by yourself?"

And Scrappy Burroughs jerks his head up, pushes back the fedora, and watches as Arthur grabs a gunny sack and starts pulling beets.

***

At the two-room schoolhouse, Anne Durham is about to embark on yet another challenge.

Poetry. She wants to teach these ragamuffin children about poetry.

She thinks, *They will not care, they will make faces, because life is hard on these plains, and who will appreciate words, even magnificent words, designed to express feeling and beauty and emotion, written to describe things that are not a part of their world?*

And she thinks some more: *That is precisely why they need to know a little poetry, to give them a glimpse of life beyond the plain, beyond the shadow of these mountains. They need to be lifted above the dry plains country, the dirt and dirty existence many of them have.*

And she feels smug, not much, but a little, because she has been to Philadelphia on several occasions, seen the Liberty Bell, and she went once to New York City, walked along Seventh Avenue, and took the ferry to Staten Island; and once to Boston, and she knows Pittsburgh as she does the back of her hand. *Most of these children*, she thinks, *have never been beyond Twin Falls, and the I.P. Falk Department Store is the biggest building they've ever seen.*

She will gently push out their boundaries with the help of Dickinson, Wordsworth, Coleridge, Tennyson, and others. It is part of her duty as a teacher. Even the youngest of them, barely beyond nursery rhymes, will benefit from this exposure to culture.

On a brittle, cold Friday morning in October, the students file in, the boys in the same denim jeans or overalls they have worn all week to school, most of the girls in the same cotton dresses they have worn all week to school, and she stands at the head of the classroom and clears her throat, pushes her eyeglasses higher on her nose, and opens a book of poetry.

She has carefully chosen a selection from Longfellow, a good American poet, and a topic they all have an interest in, snow. Certainly, these children understand something of snow, she has reasoned, and it is almost sure to catch their interest. Snow, she has deemed, is relevant.

She begins, "I am going to read you a poem today by a man named Henry Wadsworth Longfellow." The class giggles. "Yes, a funny name, I grant you that. But a fine American poet nonetheless." Eyes in the class already shoot furtive glances through the window. "I think you'll like the topic of Mr. Longfellow's poem." The class members think, *What could he write about that we'd like? Horses? Bull frogs? Pretty dresses in the window of the store? Crops? Baseball?* "His poem is about snow. I will read it to you, so please listen carefully."

With a flourish of her hand and dramatic scrubbing of her throat, she begins:

"Out of the bosom of the Air,
Out of the cloud-folds of her garment shaken"—

At this point, the older boys, the third and fourth graders, try to squelch, with little success, giggles at the mention of the words "bosom" and "garment shaken," which they all take to mean "underwear." Anne Durham is rattled but not deterred. She soldiers on. The children of this plain will have poetry, and they will have a dose of culture and, furthermore, they will like it. "*Over the woodlands brown and bare . . .*"

Anne Durham notices her, there on the first row, just off to her left. It is Mercy May Bell, sitting primly at her desk, mouthing the words a heartbeat before Anne Durham speaks them aloud.

"*Over the harvest-fields forsaken,*
Silent, and soft, and slow
Descends the snow."

Mercy May seems to be teasing her teacher. She rolls her eyes upward. She crafts a look of supreme boredom. She tugs at a curl hanging over her right ear. She makes a face at Robert Ludlow, the boy who sits across the aisle from her. And all along, she mouths the words to Longfellow's "Snow-Flakes."

Is she mocking me? thinks Anne Durham. *This Mercy May. She knows Longfellow. This little girl of the Snake River Plain. How? How can it be?*

Anne Durham finishes reading the poem, quietly closes the book, says something that makes little sense about how the class would, she hopes, someday appreciate poetry in the way she does, that poetry is art, like a good painting, and that they would read more poems together over the course of the year, and that they would become accustomed to poetry, gradually, and might even . . . and here she raises the pitch of her voice, falters because she recognizes that she is going on almost nonsensically, caterwauling, flummoxed, and thirty-three sets of young eyes are staring at her and wondering just what point their teacher is trying to make. Shaken, she glances at Mercy May, who smiles sweetly, angelically. It is as if she has cracked the teacher's code: *You thought we didn't know, you thought we couldn't know, but I do know. You are wrong, Teacher. We are smarter than you think.* And in this conceit, Mercy May is correct.

That night, in the small wood house, Anne recounts the incident to Daniel.

"I never thought that one of my students would know anything of Longfellow, much less quote him, all the while half-sneering at me," she says.

"It would be unnerving," Daniel says sympathetically, hunched over the small kitchen table, thick red pencil in hand, grading arithmetic papers. "These students of ours. They may not know much of books, of history, of culture, or mathematics. But they have grit to them. They know how to figure out things, get work done. One of my seventh-grade boys was talking about breaking down the head gasket on his family's truck the other day. Just the way you and I would speak casually about changing out a light globe."

"But this is poetry, Daniel. I never suspected. Especially from a second grader, no matter how precocious she is."

"The border of intellect doesn't stop at the Mississippi River, darling."

"No, I suppose not. Maybe I've underestimated these children."

"Maybe so. Mercy May's brothers are also very bright, although I can't imagine them mimicking poetry to me. They are rough boys but good boys. They too know how to do things."

He makes a big red check mark next to the line, "eight plus eight equals eighteen" and smiles at the irony of their discussion. Anne, who has been staring out of the south-side window of the house, staring into the darkness, looking for the first night star, wonders what else she must learn from these dusty, hard-scrabble, and practical children.

"You wanted to teach a student with promise, didn't you?" Daniel asks slyly.

"Yes, I did.

"Then maybe you've found one."

Chapter Eight

ARTHUR WORKS WITH SCRAPPY BURROUGHS to pull the last of the sugar beets and potatoes out, at least what they can before the earth freezes hard. Their hands are thick and numb from digging and pulling the tubers from the ground. Sometimes, Scrappy stuffs a dollar or two into Arthur's hands; most of the time, Arthur's help is strictly voluntary, friend to friend, brother to brother.

At night, Scrappy lies awake, his eyes fixed on a dark spot somewhere. He questions himself over and over, hundreds of times, thousands of times. When did it start to go bad? Why didn't he see it coming? What could he have done? Will his life ever be good again? What do people think of him? Why does Hill Neely's boy sleep in a warm house, have food to eat, and cash money in hand and savings in a bank, and Scrappy does not? He sleeps so little. When he arises, he is tired and stooped, and his bones ache and his head throbs and his hands are stiff and clumsy.

Three days before Thanksgiving, Arthur shoots two Canada geese on a pond above the south rim of the Snake. Not good eating, but fresh food nonetheless. He wades out into the freezing water and brings them to shore. One he keeps for himself, the other he drops off at Scrappy Burroughs's place, with nothing more said than, "We got a few of these, more 'n what we can eat. Thought you might want to take one off our hands."

Scrappy mumbles his thanks and gratefully takes the goose and shuts the door and doesn't even think to invite Arthur in. But Arthur understands and takes no offense and turns to walk the three miles back home. The son has become the father.

Second week of December, brisk and dry. Only the tops of the faraway mountains are tinged with wispy snow. The harvest was so-so; the farmers knew that by July, but it didn't matter much because prices cratered again. Each day seems to dawn the same: hard freeze, pale skies somewhere between egg blue and pearly gray, chilly winds mostly from the south and east. The days seem brittle and perturbed. Nature is out of her rhythm.

The official correspondence piles up on Scrappy Burroughs's table. He no longer reads them. He can't. The words in the letters are devastating. Only Juanita reads the letters.

She tells her husband the barest of what he needs to know: when the auction will occur, the time, what will happen. Scrappy doesn't eat much. He loses ten pounds, then five more.

His overalls sag on him. He begins to look like tattered rags upon a stick. He dreads the coming of Christmas, the first such notion in his life. He feels no peace, no joy, no goodwill. He is breaking apart a little more each day.

The final letter comes. This one he reads. He must. He reads it slowly, every word. It is the tiger at his door, and he knows he must open the door and stare eye to eye at the beast.

He instructs Juanita to find her best jewelry, her best dishes, her two Sunday dresses, and his only pair of cuff links. He pulls out the pocket watch his father gave him and a fine fountain pen, and then he mounds them all into a small wood box and digs a hole just to the east of his porch, and he buries his treasure where no sheriff's deputy or auditor from the bank will find it. He tells his four boys still at home to take what they value most and hide it in the barn.

A little pinkish color comes back to his face; he is animated, his words around the house are fiery. The sale is still on schedule: December 23. Scrappy Burroughs digs in.

Chapter Nine

PEOPLE GATHER ON A CRACKLING December night in Josephine Powell's front room.

Josephine Powell. A widow. Lost her husband, Rupert, to the Spanish flu back in 1918. She kept the farm when most people thought she'd sell out and move someplace where life was less daunting for a widow with two young sons. Even in these wrenching times, she is getting by better than most, with a little money tucked into the coffee pot, a big garden that produces more than enough, and her boys—well, they're good boys and they work hard and take things on, and they are serious and sober and devoted to their mother.

Josephine is tall and big-boned and broad through the shoulders, with hands almost the size of a Model-T headlamp and hair half silver, half brown, and big arching Joan Crawford eyebrows. She is stately. She has strength, which comes from a place beyond her physical attributes. It comes from her core, which is built in equal parts grit and compassion. Most of the bachelor farmers on the plain are a bit in love with her, but Josephine pays them no heed. She is too busy rearing her boys and making ends meet to nod toward another man's affections to even think through the maybes, what-ifs, the possibilities of a new life settling over the old one like a fresh, warm wool blanket drawn to her chin on a cold night. And she remains in love with Rupert.

But the meeting—Josephine called it. News of Scrappy Burroughs's plight raced across the plain like cheatgrass on fire. The purpose of this meeting of neighbors is simple: to determine who will buy what from the Burroughses' place, set bids that don't go sky-high, and everybody gets what they want, and the bank walks away with no more flesh than is needed.

A collusion. A cabal. A camarilla. Probably illegal, but in these days, these times, when prices are at rock bottom and the bank already owns plenty, well, you do what's best, no matter, and if the bank man walks away flummoxed and soured, so be it. So the confederacy meets. To divide the spoils, to feast upon the carrion of Scrappy Burroughs's hide. Sitting on a box is Kenneth Bailey, square built, fair-minded, sweet-natured, honest. On the floor near the stove, sitting cross-legged, whistling softly through his teeth, rocking gently, is the hermit Bowker, who whistles rather than talks and lives in a sod house close to Rock Creek. Nobody knows what his first name is and nobody is quite certain that Bowker is his true surname, and everyone is mildly surprised that he showed up because he is addled—a wild man—touched and unpredictable.

And there, just inside the doorway, near the window, is Squat Perkins, dull pocketknife in hand and whittling a piece of aspen, a man of no small temper who can be trusted only sometimes, but who knows horses better than anyone in Twin Falls County. And a dozen more, ranchers and farmers, fathers and sons, most of them barely holding on to what they have. And in walk the Andrews brothers, Tom and Ben—just kids, but holding down the farm, getting by after their father left them a few years ago, making them virtual orphans. More drift in. Good men all.

Jo Powell clears her throat and says, "I'm guessing you all know why we're here tonight. We're not trying to cheat anyone, not the bank, not Scrappy, no one. Well, maybe the bank a little, but we need to make the best of what's before us."

She shifts her weight from her left foot to her right foot. She hoists a wad of papers from the chair at her left and again glances around at the weather-beaten faces.

"Here's what's for sale at Scrappy's. I picked up this list at the courthouse." Her eyebrows rise on her forehead like tiny arched brown bridges. She balls her free hand into an enormous, strong fist. "I think it's best that we don't talk much about it and don't dally—we just get down to work and take care of who gets what. It's ugly business. But it needs to be done."

And as if on cue, as if in concert with Nature, a flash of rare December lightning shocks the evening sky and thunder bangs into the side of the house. They are only mildly superstitious, these country people, but each body in the room has the same thought.

"Maybe Scrappy knows we're here and what we're up to," says someone at the table, and nervous laughter scuffles through the room.

In the far corner of the kitchen, in a darker place, with his hat pulled low over his forehead, Arthur Bell nods in painful agreement. *Scrappy wouldn't like this,* he thinks. *He wouldn't put up with this for a minute. That man is too darn proud.*

***

The alliances are made, the prices set. The men, plus Jo Powell, shake hands and exchange nods and knowing looks. The baleful business is done, the debts pegged, the costs settled.

Arthur and his partner have claim to the prize, Scrappy Burroughs's Farmall tractor. Arthur's partner is the half-wit Bowker. It's a surprise to Arthur; as with everyone else on the plain, he figures most days Bowker is probably lucky to eat a piece of bread and a tablespoon of flour gravy, and he wonders if Bowker has the sense to mop up the gravy with his bread. After everyone has drifted out, everyone except for Arthur and Bowker, they talk, or at least they talk as much as anyone can ever claim to speak with Bowker.

Arthur says to Bowker, "We pegged the cost of the tractor at sixty dollars. I can raise fifteen or twenty dollars, but you'll need to make up the gap." And then Arthur looks at Bowker, still on the floor, still cross-legged, and Bowker whistles back to him. Arthur sees the wizened man, older-looking than his years, his nubby brown teeth currently hidden behind his straight-line lips, his blue-jelly eyes swimming. Bowker whistles continually, and some people along the plain have become proficient at deciphering just what Bowker's whistles mean. Bowker doesn't whistle with his mouth in a big round *O*; he whistles with his mouth in a straight line, wheezing out noises that don't seem to go anywhere—a dry, wispy wind with the barest trace of melody. Arthur asks Bowker the question he must: "Do you have that kind of money? If you don't, I surely don't, and we'll need a third hand. Hate to put it that way, but we need to know what we've got to work with."

Bowker glances at Arthur and whistles a high, light note. Then he looks down and deftly slides a big cigar box from around his back. He stands and opens it slowly, and Arthur is astonished by what he sees: wads of cash tied together with string, money enough to choke a mule. Bowker pulls out handfuls of it: fives and tens and twenties, and Arthur thinks there must be five hundred dollars in there easy, probably more. Bowker, it seems, is a wealthy man by the standards of the plain. Bowker changes his whistle again and grins at the flabbergasted Arthur. His whistle says, "Still worried about me? No need, brother, no need."

Slack-jawed Arthur murmurs, "Well, I guess you do have enough money. Guess we'll have ourselves a red tractor in a few days." And Bowker shyly extends a grubby hand, and the partners shake solemnly.

Bowker whistles more and nods his head and takes out forty dollars from the cigar box and hands it to Arthur. Bowker whistles in a different way, and Arthur understands with clarity: "Take this, Arthur Bell, and buy us that tractor."

Arthur nods in awe of this wrecked puzzle of a man called Bowker, and they leave Jo Powell's place as unlikely partners.

This Bowker. It is his true name, that much the people on the Snake River Plain have right. Bowker. He also has a Christian first name, Frederic. Those who are afraid of him, those who worry that he may be dangerous or violent, have no need to be. Right-minded he is not. But on the plain, there may not be a gentler, milder soul flittering about.

He came to the plain from eastern Colorado. He lives in a sod house, nearly a cave. Once, Frederic Bowker was a man of some importance to a ranching town on the broad land near the Nebraska border.

He had a wife and two children, a girl and a boy. Lost the wife in childbirth when the girl came along. Lost the girl to whooping cough when she was three. Lost the boy a year later, his one last reason for living, drowned in an irrigation canal, which for once actually had water in it. And he often thought that maybe he should end his life, too, and he came close to doing so once or twice, but something stopped him, that something being, as miserable and lonely and hard-luck bound as he seemed to be, that he would in some way be letting down his wife, their daughter, their boy. So he pushes on, unsteadily: a broken man, a broken gait, a broken life. And of course, a broken heart. But push on he does.

And through this haze of agony, Frederic Bowker had managed to sell his ranch with the help of friends who had witnessed his tragedies—one, two, and three; and he took the money he received for his land and tied it up in sturdy brown string and stuffed it in a cigar box and began to wander westward. He drifted. Most people took him for a hobo, not knowing about the cigar-box treasure. Along the way, he decided he didn't want to talk much anymore. People with good intentions always got around to asking him whether he has family, and it's too much for him to bear, much less to speak of. So he began to whistle. It seemed a prudent and practical thing to do.

To him, whistling is a logical, if odd, choice. Less talk, less pain, no explanations, no risk of an outburst of tears, no looks and nods of pity.

He is fine inside his tucked-away, soiled world, whistling to himself and, on rare occasions, to others; and he cares not that people think him a half-wit or idiot. In most respects, he prefers it that way. It is Bowker's way of dealing with a world that cannot possibly understand him.

Frederic Bowker likes a little the land he now lives on. He likes the sod house, the idea of crawling into the earth, of being part of the marl to share the feeling of lying in the soil, of being connected in that way to his buried family.

He spends his days in his hidey-hole in the ground or, when he feels like it, just wandering. When the weather gets numbing cold, or on the uncommon occasion when he feels the need of human company, he'll walk to a house, invite himself in, and just sit down. Sometimes, he visits at night when everyone in the household is asleep behind unlocked doors; more than one housewife has wakened to find Bowker curled like a baby near the stove, sleeping. It happened to Mary. The first time, she was spooked to find him asleep on her floor in the feeble light. She had gently nudged him on the shoulder.

"Mr. Bowker, would you like some breakfast?"

And Bowker had struggled up from the floor, his limbs and joints seeming to be made of stone, and whistled a long, high but pretty note, which Mary knew meant, "Yes, I'd be obliged."

After Bowker had eaten, he had put on his hat, looked toward Mary and nodded, solemnly gripped Arthur's forearm, whistled four high notes, then went outside in the brutal air to wander away the day.

At least he doesn't chew tobacco and doesn't have many stains in his coiled beard, Mary had thought, watching him hop-skip down the road.

Bowker remembers the Bell family's kindness, which he vows to someday repay. Frederic Bowker, you see, keeps a ledger of kind acts.

And now, he is a business partner of Arthur Bell, a man whom he respects. Arthur is on the debit side of Bowker's ledger; he will be repaid.

And now they will buy a tractor together from Scrappy Burrows. Arthur and Bowker. Partners. At the thought of it, Bowker begins a whistle, a high, shrill, bouncy, happy whistle whooshing from a man who has had precious little in life to be joyful about.

Later that night, Arthur crawls into bed next to Mary. He kisses her on the forehead and twists a strand of her hair. She sleepily asks, "How'd it go?"

"Purty well. Me and Bowker are going to buy the tractor."

Mary sits up in bed, sleep chased from her like fall leaves before a stout wind.

"Mr. Bowker? The man who whistles and doesn't talk?" The night seems to grow even chillier, and there is a blue iciness in Mary's tone as she rips the blanket toward her and turns her back on her husband. "Arthur. Do you know what you're doing?"

He turns the question over in his head, ruffles it a bit, and gives an honest answer, which is the only answer a guileless man such as Arthur can give.

"No, Mary, I'm not quite sure I do."

***

The sale day arrives. Much of what Scrappy and Juanita Burroughs own will be in the hands or house of someone else by early afternoon.

It is four in the morning, and Scrappy Burroughs is up. He paces in the kitchen. He drinks bitter coffee. The wind nips at the west side of the house, and the house creaks like an old wood ship sailing across a squally ocean. He dresses. He puts on his best shirt, his Sunday shirt. He puts on a good pair of trousers, and of course he puts on the battered fedora. Today will lift him up and drop him to the ground. It will grind him, tear him, cause him to wince in misery.

But he will look dignified and act dignified and talk dignified. Christmas is two days away. With all calamity hurled at him, he is determined to hold firm. What he fears most is this: at the end of the day, in their homes that night, fire embers popping, husbands and wives tucked under their blankets to fight the chill will talk. And they will say, "How did he make out, how'd he do?" and the answer could be, "He didn't look good, looked done in. Poor Scrappy."

He will have none of that talk.

First light. A raw west wind blows and heavy, ash-colored clouds scud across the sky. A few minutes before eight, Scrappy Burroughs reaches for his coat and stands on his front porch to greet Sheriff Prater and Hill Neely's son and whoever else might be coming to oversee the picking of his bones.

***

Nobody hardly speaks. Scrappy Burroughs notices right off. He catches a few glances, a few nods, an awkward "hullo" in the bitter air. *So,* thinks Scrappy, *this is how it is. It's like telling someone you got cancer or your wife left you for a traveling shoe salesman or your boy got caught stealing a horse. They don't know how to take it. They don't know what to say. It's as if you were a leper,* he thinks.

There are maybe fifty people in the yard. The auctioneer, a man brought in by the bank, is dressed in a heavy coat and string tie and talks in a staccato, rat-tat-tat style. He's a jumpy sort, eyes darting, quick to read the crowd, quick to sight the smallest of movements. *He is like a nighthawk,* thinks Scrappy, *prowling for prey in the dim light of evening.*

Nearby is Edgar Neely, the banker, dressed in a suit and wooly overcoat, looking smug. He has a couple of young toadies with him, there to do whatever he instructs. He remains a man small in spirit and heart; he has not forgotten the scene in the bank when Scrappy Burroughs went off like a fiery pinwheel, spewing invective in front of the bank patrons.

Today, Edgar Neely will have his revenge. Today, he will take almost everything Scrappy Burroughs owns, including his pride. Sheriff Prater leans against a porch post, although Scrappy figures he's disgusted by the whole affair and imagines the lawman would much rather be chasing gin smugglers out of Canada or be hot on the trail of bank robbers. Taking what a good man owns at the behest of the bank is not what he was elected to do, or so imagines Scrappy. The theory is confirmed moments later when the sheriff grabs Scrappy's hand and says, "Sorry 'bout the way things turned out for ya. Sorry to be here. Don't like much that runt of a banker."

The bidding begins. First, tools from the barn. Scrappy wonders at the penurious bids. Three pennies for a planer. A nickel for the saw. A nice wrench. A good hammer. A set of files. Fifty cents for the bunch.

Hill Neely's son looks bewildered. He whispers something to a toady, who nods his head and bustles off into the crowd. The corners of Sheriff Prater's mouth bend in a long, slow, knowing smile. He pops a toothpick in his mouth. *May yet have some fun today,* he thinks.

Scrappy Burroughs falls into dark contemplation about his friends and neighbors.

Six milk cans come up for bid, and a toady flicks his hand in the air and says, "Five dollars." The auctioneer's nippy eyes scan the farmyard, and he seems gratified. He begins working the crowd, working the farmers to jack up the price, in his rat-tat-tat speaking style. Maybe that bid will warm up this crowd of beat-up folks and they'll start digging deeper into their pockets. Or so he hopes, because his payday is pegged squarely to how much he can coax out of these bent and poorly folks.

But such is not the case. The men remain silent. The auctioneer, exasperated, asks for more bids, pleads with the crowd, cajoles and bullies, appeals to their pride as men, as Americans, as God-fearing stewards of the land, but no more bids come. The wind shanks a new way, from the northwest, and from a black-and-purple cloud, pebbly graupel stings the sides of men's faces. And the bid for the milk cans stands pat at five dollars. And the toady is the puzzled owner of six milk cans, though he's likely never touched a cow's udder in his lifetime.

Hill Neely's son explodes in anger. He rushes to the sheriff and cups his hand and fumes, "Can't you see what's happening, Sheriff? They've all got together and rigged the prices. They are cheating the bank."

Sheriff Prater listens and nods, wise as Solomon, patient as Job. He sees the Andrews twins a few feet away.

"Ben Andrews. The bank man here says you and the others got together and fixed all the prices amongst yourselves. It's called collusion and might not be right with the law, so I guess I'm obliged to ask. Are y'all fixing the prices?"

"No sir," says Ben Andrews with saccharine innocence while his brother Tom solemnly pumps his head up and down in agreement. "Me and Tom wouldn't do that. We want the bank people to be happy because they've been so good to us through the years."

And Sheriff Prater says, "Didn't think so." He turns to Hill Neely's son, who is red in the face and looks far less smug than an hour ago, and says, "There isn't no price fixing, Edgar. Known the Andrews boys their whole lives, and they wouldn't lie to me," he says while thinking, *Unless they had good cause to, which is the case today.*

Hill Neely's son sits down on the porch, pale, trembling, and holds his chin in his hands and curses these simple farm people who have outsmarted him.

The bigger items come along—discs and harrows, wheelbarrows, pumps, irrigation pipes, household furniture, saddles, and other livery goods. Then comes one of the prizes, Scrappy Burroughs's favorite horse, a gentle dapple mare named Cheeky, and she goes to the Andrews twins for eight dollars. Every transaction is completed with one bid, and one bid only—neat, orderly, efficient.

The men in the crowd say nothing to each other, their faces stony, their hands thrust deep into their pockets, their feet pawing the ground. They have ugly business to take care of, and they are masterful. They act with the precision of trained assassins. Jo Powell permits herself a slow, satisfied smile.

Even Squat Perkins perfectly plays his role, scowling while he offers three dollars for a tractor rake.

From his porch, Scrappy Burroughs watches with both warmth and building fury. It pains him to see what he has gained through a lifetime of toil whisked away for pennies on the dollar. He understands. But he doesn't understand. His neighbors, people he has helped through hard times, have become as cruel and calculating as the bank. He is being picked clean, not by people he considers ravens and vultures but by songbirds.

They are not songbirds, he decides. He is a man in powerful conflict and does indeed feel like a dying lamb in the field, looking up as the birds of prey slowly loop overhead then dive with talons exposed toward the helpless animal bleating in the sea of sage and grass. Cheeky, for eight dollars. Cheeky. Good boys, those Andrewses. But. His face registers no pain, yet he is a broken man, every bone inside him snapping with every item put up for auction.

Then comes the biggest prize of the day, the Farmall. The auctioneer, frazzled and just wanting to finish his business and get away from this nightmare of a place, opens the bidding.

Near the front of the knot of men, Arthur says, "Sixty dollars." A dozen yards away, Bowker grins and whistles and does a hop-step in the dirt.

"I have sixty . . . what more, who more, come on, I need eighty, I need eighty, somebody give me . . ." He seethes. He almost spits out his words.

No one says a word. No one moves a muscle. The slashing graupel stops its earthbound descent, and a thin shaft of sunlight touches the earth to the east of Scrappy Burroughs's house.

Silence. Only silence.

The auctioneer slumps, and the bravado in his voice wilts. He smiles ruefully and says, "Gents, I know when I've been outsmarted. To the victors," he says wanly. "Sold for sixty."

Bowker and Arthur, an unlikely pair, have taken on the mighty bank, and they have won.

Bowker whistles with glee, turns, and starts the long walk back to his sod house, back to the soil, where the earth will swallow him up, keep him warm, and act as a companionable angel on this happy day.

***

It is over for Scrappy Burroughs. He has faced the worst he can imagine, save for the loss of Juanita or a son, and he has survived the savagery. And he survived in his best shirt and his best pants and his fedora, and he didn't tremble and he didn't yelp and he didn't show a sign of failing, no matter the rage within.

And that night, when couples turn in, and the woman looks to the man and asks, "So how'd Scrappy Burroughs take it all?" he gets his wish. The men of the plain all say something close to the same: "He took things well. Yes, it was a strain, how could it not be? But he's got the Burroughs mettle. He'll figure a way out of it."

Which is not to say that later that night, as Scrappy thinks about all that is gone, all that is lost, and most of all how none of his friends hardly nodded or gestured to him in any way, that he would not stand on his front porch and look at a weak quarter-moon in the now-clear night air and howl. He howls like a wolf, howls like a wounded animal, howls from his depths, howls because of white, raging despair, and questions the course and worth of life itself.

Juanita comes at midnight, wool blankets in hand, drapes them over the big slumped shoulders of her husband, swaddles him, and goes inside without a word. She knows Scrappy needs to be alone this night, just him and the cold quarter-moon and the slats of the porch and tattered remains of what once was his. Joy to the world, none. Silent night, yes—too silent as it turns out. *Some Christmas,* he thinks acridly. Some Christmas indeed.

***

It is just after first light when Scrappy hears the noise. He lifts himself up from the porch, lost, his spirit spent in rage and sorrow, half dead, stiff and sore, his back creased from the wood slats. He catches his own odor—rank, salty, masculine.

Clanky, clanky, clanky. Roaring, the slip of gears, the grinding transmission, someone not familiar with the machine. A puff of vapid blue-white smoke in the distance. The clanking grows, and it is familiar to him. He knows that sound. He knows that engine.

It is the Farmall. *His* Farmall. *His* tractor. Which he no longer owns.

Who? What? Why? On the day before Christmas.

And as his vision clears and his senses regain their footing, a wondrous scene is unveiled: It is Bowker, the madman. He is driving the Farmall toward the house. Bowker, with his hands flying, whistling mostly drowned by the tractor's noise, then cackling as triumphant as a conquering Roman general in a victory procession. It is Bowker the half-wit, laughing, flapping his arms in the air, and almost wiggling a dance in the seat of the tractor. The sight spawns in Scrappy a thin smile, and he wonders how Bowker keeps the tractor on the road.

And alongside him, half-trotting, grinning almost as crazily as Bowker, is Arthur.

Scrappy is stunned and cannot think or move. He simply watches the addled Bowker slowly drive the tractor into the front yard. Juanita, hearing the familiar clank and roar, seeing the puff of bluish smoke, comes to the porch and grabs Scrappy's hands, and the tears well in her eyes, and then they gush in the bitter Christmas Eve air, and the tears freeze on her face, spicy sparkly diamonds, as Bowker stops the tractor and hops down, whistling like the fool some people take him to be. She sees it all. She sees what is happening. She understands her neighbors' silence the morning before. They *had* to be silent. They *had* stood by her family.

She says, "Oh, Scrappy! They're back! Our friends are back! Sweet merciful Christmas, our friends are back!" And then something so magnificent happens that Scrappy, Juanita, and Arthur can scarcely believe it. Bowker leaps down and hands Scrappy the key to the tractor, and then he speaks—words—through a crooked grin, jelly eyes dancing, head swaying, specks of food lodged in his wire-brush beard. And when he speaks, he speaks in a deep-throated, mellifluous voice, the most implausible happening of any in the unbelievable short chain of events.

"Scrappy Burroughs, agin it's your'n."

And with that, Bowker takes a step back, turns around, starts whistling, and hops and jigs and bounces happily toward his earthen home, so many miles away.

Scrappy Burroughs cannot think of a thing to say, not a word, no, not a word. He just stands there with the key in his hand, stunned, bewildered, overwhelmed, watching the flappy figure of Bowker grow smaller against the blue-cold morning horizon.

There is more here than a man who gets back his tractor. So much more, not the least of which is this: Bowker feels redeemed. Partway, leastwise. He never has shucked the feeling that he was responsible, somehow, for the tragedy of his family. On this day, he might have given life back to another family standing at the edge of a mawing chasm.

Here is a man who held his wife as she died in their bed, died in a surge of warm, thick blood while bringing a child into the world. Here is a man who held his young daughter as she passed, helplessly held her as her wheezing and pain-wracked lungs finally simpered and fell silent. Here is a man who pitifully tried to blow back the breath of life into the blue-lipped body of his waterlogged son, screaming, "Lazarus!" though the boy's name was Abel. Here is a man who has known pain and anguish and regret and remorse almost each moment of his adult life. Here is a man who buried himself in a home in the soil, hiding from all that has happened to him, asking in crude prayer to be taken too—taken to where *they* are. He has punished himself for years, punished himself until it did make him sick and a little crazy. But today. This act. For a moment, the sorrow eases.

Doesn't each man deserve to lie in his bed at night and think of the good he has done? Something so good as to be intractable, something that helps to plane the humpy terrain of sorrow and misery and despair and doubt that good men sometimes feel?

For Bowker, it comes in the form of restoring a tractor to Scrappy Burroughs. From a broken man, in a bold, kind attempt to keep another from breaking.

As the day goes on, neighbors drift by, returning all they purchased the day before. The Andrews brothers lead Cheeky, the dappled mare, to Scrappy. "Tried to ride her," says Ben Andrews, "but she wouldn't have no part of us." Tom Andrews finishes the thought: "You spoilt her. High-strung. Spooky." And in unison, the twins say, "She's yours," and turn toward home.

And Ken Bailey comes by, bringing a wagonload of goods, including six milk cans.

"Saw the young feller who was at the auction with Hill Neely's boy yesterday afternoon. Asked him if he knew where I could buy any milking cans. Wasn't too happy, but he sold 'em to me anyway. A buck and a quarter. I figure the bank came out on the short end. Felt purty good."

In the end, it's Arthur who says what needs to be said to Scrappy Burroughs.

"We had to be careful and not let the bank catch wind of what we were up to. We knew if you figured out what we were doing, you'd have put your foot down and stopped us. You're prideful, Scrappy, in case no one has told you.

"You'd have done the same for us. You already *have* done so much for us. We're happy to neighbor with you." And Scrappy Burroughs looks down and shuffles his feet a bit and recognizes what Arthur says is true. Even the part about being prideful.

A good man such as Scrappy Burroughs doesn't need much. He doesn't think he's bigger or better than anyone else, nor stronger or smarter. He rises early, he works hard at whatever chores the day brings him, he takes care of his family, he takes care of his friends. He doesn't want any notice and hardly any thanks. He doesn't need to ask what's right or wrong.

He just knows. It's what makes people decent. And Scrappy Burroughs, far more than most, is a decent man.

And this particular Christmas Eve night, lying in the big feather bed, Juanita looks at Scrappy, and he pulls her stout, strong body to him, and he says in a voice so soft it surprises her, "We're Burroughses. We're strong. We'll be okay. We'll figure it out."

And in a sod house, not far from the lip of the Snake River Canyon, Frederic Bowker settles into his crude wood cot. He whistles a little, a tune that sounds a bit like a carol, maybe "Away in a Manger." He smiles himself to sleep.

And when Christmas dawns, this is what is found on the plain:

Two men.

Neighbors.

Redemption.

Scrappy Burroughs was right after all. It was, indeed, some Christmas.

Chapter Ten

THE GLOW OF HELPING SCRAPPY Burroughs retain most of what he owns sweeps the little community on the south side of the Snake into Christmas. The temperatures drop below zero at night; the relentless wind groans and stings to the core of the few who venture outdoors. Then, in a single afternoon, the clear skies turn slate and dour. They take on a dark, shapeless gray, and the snow begins. It snows for two days. Eighteen inches pile up. It is a time to stay close, stay inside, stay warm, stay alive. Life slows to a tentative, plodding pace, gripped in winter's icy fist.

Anne and Daniel Durham decide to ride out the Christmas vacation in the small house far from the comforts of their East Coast homes. Then one night, the wind pounds harder than ever and the powdery snow wedges in through the cracks around the doors and windows, and Anne spends a long chattery night, and no amount of blankets can warm her; not the blankets, not her coat, not hot-water bladders, not Daniel's body when he snugs up to her and puts his thick arms around her. And in the sketchy gray dawn, chilled and rattled, she looks at Daniel and says, "Let's go home. I need to feel carpet under my feet and heat in a house," and Daniel nods with conviction and says, "Yes, we'll go home for the break." And he wonders if he will ever get Anne to come back, but he thinks she will return, and that indeed proves to be the case. They spend Christmas Eve on a train somewhere in southern Illinois; dead cornstalks plowed under, lining both sides of the track; brown, bare oak trees waving them home; rushing and clacking by flickering light from hobo campfires licking up from each trestle they cross.

Bowker the hermit stays in his earthen home and sleeps much of the day and sees no one. He eats an apple in the afternoon and a tin of fish in the evening. Christmas day comes and passes, and he takes little note, offers no warmth, and receives none in return. Then, late that night, he remembers, remembers it is the birth of the Christ, and he pulls his mouth back wide and pushes his jaw forward, and if you were outside of the sod dugout, you would hear a humble man again whistling a song; this time, it sounds more than a bit like "O Little Town of Bethlehem." It is his way of noting the day, a fine expression of honor because it is heartfelt. No gifts, no decorated trees, no gaudy lights or festive supper. Just a lone man remembering and whistling, and it may be the purest Christmas celebration on the plain. He thinks of his wife and his girl, and he thinks a little more about his boy because on this December day, much of the world thinks of a newborn son. He thinks of the tractor and the look on Scrappy Burroughs's face and gives a whoop of glee that rumbles through his sod home, spills outdoors, and fades to nothingness on the dark, cold plain. Bowker knows that, despite the pain he feels with every breath, God loves him, and many of His children on the South Plain do too. For Bowker, it is enough.

Hill Neely's son sits in the parlor of his house and contemplates the bright Christmas tree, fluttery candles, the fine big gifts bunched under its boughs. He thinks venomously of the humble people of the plain, convincing himself that they really didn't outsmart him; no, rather, they broke the law and that's the only way they could have come out ahead of him and the bank. In a fair fight, he would have won. And he thinks, too, that those same people were likely cold in their houses this very moment, burning smelly juniper or dirty coal in their stoves, the children playing with a few crude, homemade toys; for their gifts, a piece of fruit, maybe; sticks of cheap peppermint candy and weak apple cider. And the thought of what he mistakenly believes to be their suffering and deprivation brings him odd, cold comfort. He never once considers a baby born in humble circumstances in a faraway town as the reason everyone pauses this day and rejoices. He remains a small man.

And what Hill Neely's son could never picture or imagine it, but the bank he works for, the bank touted as the best in Idaho with the most cash reserves west of the Divide, the bank directed by the best minds in that part of the country, the stone edifice that has become part of his very soul, will collapse in little more than a year, and he will be out of work for many months before finding a job at a lumber yard at half the wage the bank paid him. And it will cause a part of him to wither and die, but it is a part of him that is better off dead.

Hill Neely's son never will be a good man, much less a great man, but his ability to lord over others will be diminished for the remainder of his life. Some people need to let the ill part of their nature die, die, and just bury it and find new life elsewhere. Edgar Neely is among them.

But there are few of the likes of Hill Neely's son on the Southern Idaho Plain. The playful, bighearted, lusty Andrews twins, well, they've set a few dollars aside somehow, and they go into Twin and buy small toys at I. P. Falk's and a few mittens and a few scarves, and they creep up to homes on the Eve, where they know there are both children and hard times, and they leave their gifts at the door and knock hard and then run like flighty deer across the snow and dive over a mounded bank and wait, their breath hanging frozen and foggy in the chill brittle air; and they listen to the clamor and boisterous voices and the happy, sobbing shouts into the black night sky, "Look! Santa has been here! Thank ye! Whoever ye be, thank ye, and God bless! Merry Christmas to ye!" And lying on the snow, they grin and punch each other, and it doesn't matter that the night air is chilly and their life-breath comes forth in a kind of vapory fog; they are happy, and they are warm in ways that matter most.

And Scrappy Burroughs, for him it is a Christmas always to remember, and in some ways the best; he has few gifts, only oranges for his boys and a small bracelet made of agates for Juanita—a bracelet he made himself, with little stones he found and polished—and when he gives it to her, she says, "Oh, Scrappy. Thank you. It is so beautiful. We have so much." And all the Burroughses sit together on Christmas Eve, and they sing carols and they find that gifts sometimes only get in the way of what is truly important and what they should remember.

Scrappy lumbers around the house after everyone else has retired; he pokes the ashes of the fireplace, he rubs the peels of the oranges between his big, bearish hands, and he holds his hands to his face and takes a long deep breath, savoring the tangy aroma; and he looks out of his window to see if the firmament is clear and then searches for the brightest star in the sky.

And then he walks onto his porch and breathes the sharp, pungent air, and he sits down on the slats, the place where only a night ago he slept in rough misery, and thinks of friends and good fortune and he ushers in Christmas Day, right there, tears snaking down his cheeks. Though he goes to church because Juanita insists, and though he does not consider himself a religious man, at this moment, Scrappy believes, believes in something higher, something bigger, something more compassionate and loving than reason alone can explain. He sees one star sparkling brighter than any other, and he nods at it. He nods, and across the frozen, silent sage, he hears a carol earnestly sung by a family who lives a mile away, because sound carries far on the plain on cold, crackling nights.

And right there on the porch, he softly sings along with his neighbor family, "Far, Far Away on Judea's Plains," though he knows nobody can hear him, and maybe it's best that way, because Scrappy Burroughs sings akin to noise made by gravel being stirred with a stick in a rusty bucket.

Arthur and Mary retire early on Christmas Eve. Days before, Arthur talked Mary into dipping into the sugar bowl for three dollars—"It is Christmas. We'll

make it up soon enough; times are getting a little better, Mary."—and he has a
penknife for Lucas, a whistle for Samuel, a wool hat for Silas, three big marbles—
one blue, one white, one red—for James Richard, and a little hair clip for Mercy
May—a small gift to be sure, one that he saw in a glass case in Mr. Sperry's store
and knew right away he wanted for his daughter. He had not seen the price on
the first or second or third approach to the glass case, but on the fourth trip, he
cleared his throat and asked Mr. Sperry how much it cost, and though the answer
was a dollar, Mr. Sperry, who had three daughters of his own and knew the feeling
of a father for his girls and could see the wanting and hope all etched over the face
of Arthur Bell, said, "That one is twenty-five cents, Arthur. It's a good buy. It'd
look mighty nice on a young girl."

And Arthur was relieved and tried not to show too much excitement, so he
just said, "Well, in that case, I believe I'll take it, Mr. Sperry. I believe that will
make a fine gift for my girl. You know my girl, Mercy May?"

And Mr. Sperry nodded and said, "Yes, I do. You've only got the one girl,
I recollect. It has to be her. Cute little thing, Arthur. And you probably wanted
another boy at one time."

And for Mary, he buys a little soft towel from Mr. Sperry. He thinks she will
like it. It is a sky blue and adds color to their drab home and furnishings. He
doesn't know exactly what the towel is for. It is too small to be a bath towel and
too large to be a washcloth. But it is new and smells fresh, like a good breeze in
April, and it is soft, and he thinks, *Maybe it is a holding towel, just a towel to hold,
because it is soft and so much of what Mary does each day is so hard and coarse. That
is what it will be: Mary's holding towel.*

So this Christmas comes and goes along the south side of the Snake River
Plain. The troubles and the woes, the hard days now that certainly will lead to hard
times in weeks to come, are temporarily turned away; and small things become
large things and important things and things that are remembered—the tang of
orange peels; the lung-bursting sprint of young men across a dark, snowy field
and their attempts to shunt away crackly laughter; a shopkeeper with daughters,
who understands their need to feel pretty; the sound of mostly off-key family
choirs singing Christmas carols as the cold, pale sun eases toward the western
skyline; the tears of a thankful man who is not religious but who nonetheless has
the faith to gaze at the clear night sky in search of a twinkly star; a blue towel just
for holding; and the rattling, wispy whistle of a man who lives under the ground
and cackles with joy at the thought of his charity.

Mercy May places the hair clip on the side of her head.

Lucas solemnly opens the two blades of his penknife and quietly folds them
back into place.

Samuel softly blows into his whistle.

Silas tries on his new cap and looks in the only mirror in the house.

James Richard rolls his marbles in his hands over and over and over.

Mary caresses her blue towel.

Arthur allows himself a moment to feel pleased, for even during these ragged times, he has provided for his family.

Christmas night, after all have retired, the moon strains against clouds that drift over the plain from the west. The diaphanous moonlight seems to quiver and shake, and then it disappears, prescribed to a dark heaven. By morning, the large gray cotton-bellied clouds are spitting snow, and the temperature plummets and the wind makes a groaning, throaty sound as it rips through leafless trees.

Christmas has come: peaceful, sweet, warm. And then it leaves. Winter has come again.

Chapter Eleven

THE RUG AT THE END of her soft, fluffy bed. The plastered pastel walls. The graceful light fixtures. The pantry filled with food. The delicate, lacy curtains on the windows. The warm blowing air from a furnace. The comfort of family and friends, of people calling upon each other. And no outhouses. Indoor plumbing, enough to make her feel pampered, a queen. And while the Pennsylvania weather is cold, there is no shrill, biting wind, not like that of the Snake River Plain in faraway Idaho. Idaho. Was she really there, or was it all a long and complicated dream?

Anne Durham revels in being home.

For two whole days she glories in her parents' plush house, and through breakfast on the third.

Then she is surprised at how much she thinks about her schoolchildren. She tells people of them, their stories, their hardships, how they ride horses to school, how many of them wear the same threadbare clothing each day. She tells how some families disappear overnight, never to be heard of again. She tells them of her prized students, especially the small spitfire named Mercy May, who can recite Longfellow and Dickinson as effortlessly as her multiplication tables. She tells how she cannot eat in front of the children because she knows many have had little more than a slice of bread, a potato, or tomatoes canned the previous fall. She tells them of children who arise before dawn to milk cows, who work long hours in the fall with gunny bags tied to their rope belts to bring in the sugar beets and potatoes, or spuds, as they're called in the West, laughing at the moniker as she says it to family and friends. Spuds. Such a funny word!

She tells them of seeing a mountain lion on a walk in the foothills one October evening and feebly tries to describe the way the sun rises over the Albions to the east, how the light is so long and thin and takes on hues that she has never seen before, colors without names.

No, Idaho was not a dream. It is real to her. Real and enduring and lovely, and it tugs at her emotions. And she thinks how she has never felt quite so alive as on those chilly mornings on the south side of the Snake, especially on Saturdays, when she is prone to taking a long walk.

And her mother, after listening well into the evening to her speak of these Idaho people and places, reaches across the kitchen table and takes Anne's hands into her own and says softly, "It sounds as though you've found a home and found a place, dear Anne. It sounds as though you have found people to love. How strange it is that you were led to Idaho. I am happy for you, but I will miss you and Daniel. I know now that you will never be back, except as a visitor, and I must accept that. Oh my, but how you have grown."

Anne throttles a protest and thinks, "Mother is right. I have my place, and Daniel has his, too." And soon she aches for her return to Idaho, to greet her students, to help them pull off mittens, to hang raggedy coats near the stove to dry, to gather them close to her and teach, just teach, because the joy of sharing knowledge is all she wants to do with her life. She looks forward to spring and the wonders of a land that soon will renew itself and what she will learn in the season of happy change. And she understands her mother is correct: she has found a people to love and a place where she can feel peace.

And the long train ride back to Idaho seems a triumphant return, and her heart thumps and pulses fast and hard as she looks outside the window and sees places familiar to her. Daniel squeezes her hand as the train grinds to a stop at Twin Falls and says, "Well, we are here, and it is our home now. We both know that. Home. Home in Idaho. I am surprised at the strangeness of it all. How peculiar is the way Providence works!"

Daniel hires a man to drive them to their crackerbox house, and Anne soaks in the snowy view, remembering the faces that belong in the small stone or wood houses she passes and trying to tamp down the excitement she feels at the thought that, in two days, her students will file in, red fire in their cheeks from the bitter cold, crinkly blue veins against the milk-white skin of their hands, eyes wide with wonder at what she will say, what she will teach them.

Anne Durham is from Pennsylvania, but now Idaho is her home.

Chapter Twelve

THE WARMTH OF THE CHRISTMAS season can no longer hold back winter from its due, and winter soon follows its natural form and spares no one. January is brutal, cruel, and bitter. Winter's claw touches the mountains on all sides of the plain and down into the Snake River basin, painting the landscape in deep, white, drifted snow. The wind blows mostly from the north and west, sometimes carrying frigid Arctic air to Idaho. From the drafty teachers' house, Daniel and Anne send word home with their students to the parents: *If you can, send a spare blanket, send it with your children, in case a blizzard bellows and your children need to spend a night or two in the schoolhouse because the danger is too great to send them home. All blankets will be carefully catalogued and names attached.* When the rattling grip of winter eases, they will be returned to the families who shared them.

Daniel and Anne both understand that what they ask is no small favor, that some families have no blankets to spare and probably not enough to keep children warm within their houses to begin with. They tell the children to make sure they say that blankets to school are optional, loaned only if they could be spared. Anne frets. She twists and turns and huddles against Daniel in those bitter January nights and thinks how cold some of her students must be. The north wind groans and tatters against the bare trees and sage. Coffee leftover from the night before freezes in its pot before the next morning. Anne writes her parents about the paucity of blankets, and to her surprise and joy, a huge box shows up in the mail three weeks later with small brown wool blankets. Her gratitude rises as an ocean swell, and she understands again that her family comprehends her choice of profession and place and husband too.

In the Bell home, Mary listens to the message from Mercy May and Lucas, and later that night, quietly pulls one of the two blankets from her bed, folds it, and sets it on the kitchen table, where the children will see it and will take it to school. She and Arthur can wear their day clothes over their night clothes.

They can draw close to each other. They can heat stones and put them under the remaining blanket. They will get by.

There is little work at this time of year, but there is time for the occasional visit, when people summon the will to go outdoors and wrap themselves up against the chill elements and venture forth.

Scrappy Burroughs sets out on a rare blue-skied, crackling cold morning to visit Arthur. He knocks gingerly on the front door, partly from politeness, partly to spare his hand from the sting of pulpy flesh on cold hardwood in temperatures flirting with zero.

"Mornin', Mary," he says when she answers the door. And he takes off his wool winter hat and scrapes his shoe across the door jamb and wishes he were someone else, almost anywhere else, with the message he has to deliver.

"Why, Scrappy. Come on in. I suppose it's Arthur you want to see."

Scrappy nods and says, "Yes," and Mary motions him to a wood chair in the kitchen.

"Coffee? Something to warm you up, Scrappy?" And he shakes his big head and mumbles, "No, thanks, Mary."

Arthur comes into the kitchen, wiping his hands on a rag that he's been using to clean some of his hand tools. Winter work. He looks at Scrappy's face and sees the worry lines, the crinkly blue folds of skin under his eyes, and thinks, *They weren't there last summer.*

This is a solemn occasion; Mary feels it, knows it, and without a word, disappears into the house's other downstairs room and stands in the far corner and puts her hands to her ears and thinks that the winter has been too long and it's still just January; and she wonders if she's getting soft in some way because she can't remember cold and wind and slate-gray countryside and poor prospects ever bothering her so much before. She drops her hands and smooths the sides of her dress and tries not to listen to the muffled voices in the kitchen.

Scrappy listlessly says hello to Arthur and then gets to the heart-weary purpose of his visit. "I come to talk with you about the spring."

Arthur nods and says, "I figured as much."

And Scrappy says, "I kept you on for as long as I could last fall, but you know as well as anyone that I could barely feed my own. And you kept coming, even when you knew you wouldn't get paid, and for that, I am grateful to you."

Arthur says, "It's all right, Scrappy. You'd've done the same for me if our places were switched."

Scrappy says, "I would have, and I am glad to know you think that."

The two men sit in silence for a few seconds. Scrappy shifts uneasily in his chair. Outside, a cloud blows in front of the sun and a muted shadow swarms over the land. Scrappy wonders if this is a sign or if his mind is conjuring too much. Arthur drums his fingers on the table. In the next room over, Mary's fingers are intertwined and twitchy.

"Should be a good water year. With all this snow," Arthur finally says. "That'll be nice."

"Yep." Scrappy looks out the window and feels as if he is going to be sick. "We need it. Need it bad."

"But you've come to tell me something, Scrappy, and I bet I already know. No work this spring, true enough?"

And Scrappy, hoarse and suddenly flushed in the face, says only, "True enough," and it seems as though a dagger has been plunged into his chest.

Arthur raises his eyes and thinks hard. He hadn't really expected work from Scrappy Burroughs, but he had hoped, had hoped hard, that maybe something would turn up right, what with the good water year, and F. D. R. making speeches about new deals and fair deals and government camps sprouting up here and there, and besides, how could all of this bad luck and bad times go on anyway? Things had to break. Things couldn't go on like this forever. Things had to break for the better sometime.

He thinks of Mary and the boys, and he thinks of Mercy May, and he does the quick calculations of a desperate man, and like all good men who are desperate, like all people who are reduced to almost nothing, he concludes, *We'll find a way. We'll get by. We'll do something.*

And Scrappy Burroughs, still numb, across from him, not knowing what to say. Maybe the two words, "true enough," are the entire message he needs to convey. He knows what he tells Arthur comes as no surprise, but surprise or not, bad news is never easy to spit out to a friend, never something to look forward to saying.

And what does Arthur think of him? This is an important consideration to Scrappy Burroughs. Arthur, whom he looks upon as a younger brother. Arthur, the man of all men he least wants to disappoint. Arthur, the man whom Scrappy depends on for approval and, in some way that he cannot explain and would even loathe to think, the man whose opinion he values the most. Scrappy Burroughs who has been a protector and a rescuer all of his life, but lately, he has not only been unable to perform those cherished duties but has had to rely on others to help pull him through. He thinks, *I did not know this was coming. I did not know it would be this way. I am surprised and disappointed and feel as if I am less a man.* And all of this coming to him as he sits in the kitchen of Arthur Bell's small home and tells him there wouldn't likely be any work come March, when work is supposed to come. And he couldn't even quite do that; the words would not come, and it remained up to Arthur to speak, to plug in the gaps, to tell himself his own sour news.

Arthur sits in the chair, and he thinks, and he calculates, and he figures some more, and he mentally drifts away for a few minutes, away from the house, away from the brutal cold of the Snake River Plains, away from, it seems, the earth itself.

And his thoughts parallel those of his friend Scrappy Burroughs, which sometimes happens when two men know each other better than brothers. *This is all harder than I thought it would be*, he thinks, and with that, he lifts his shoulders and lets them down, and he looks across the table at Scrappy, and he knows what he needs to do. He thinks, *I need to be a good fellow right now. I can push Scrappy over, but I won't. None of this is worth risking Scrappy's friendship, and look at him; Scrappy seems ready to weep, and he is broken, and there's no use in both of us being dragged down any further than we already are. Scrappy's been broke once already last fall and we put him back together, but I don't know we could do it again.*

So Arthur acts with grace and kindness, which isn't surprising; it's his nature, anyway.

"I understand," Arthur says, his faint Tennessee drawl surfacing in the deliberate pace of his speech. "It's kind of the way I figured it would be, so I was planning ahead a bit, and we'll be fine, very fine, so don't you and Juanita or no one else start to worrying."

Scrappy Burroughs nods and says, "Okay, and I thank you, and if something turns around, I'll be at your door. You're the first man I'll put on. Even for piecework."

"Thank you, Scrappy."

The hard business is done. Scrappy is relieved and sorrowful and confused and a little bit angry, although at what he cannot tell. Just circumstances, things he can't control: the weather, people who plowed up the plains, Hoover, banks, the middlemen who jacked up prices for transport of crops, the farmers' co-op that didn't do much for him. All of them and more.

Arthur understands his friend and knows that he needs to say something or do something to let Scrappy Burroughs grasp that nothing has changed between them. He wants to leave his friend whole, even though his friend's news has not been good. Arthur doesn't need to think, doesn't need to form the words in his mind, but he instinctively understands, in such circumstances, this is what a gentleman and friend does.

Scrappy stands and trundles toward the door, his big feet thumping on the wood floor, and reaches for the handle and opens it. He puts on his hat and rubs his hands together and then turns when Arthur calls him, the moment when Arthur tosses him the sinewy rope that will pull Scrappy toward him, the rope that Arthur will use to pull his friend toward shore and home port.

Arthur says, "Something I never have known. Been kind of a puzzle to me but never asked. It's this. What's your given birth name, Scrappy? Never have known and wanted to ask several times, even talked once about it once or twice with Mary. It's your name. You aren't truly a Scrappy, are you?"

Scrappy looks embarrassed and shifts his weight uneasily and pushes back his hat and sighs and says, "No. My real name is Julius." And he expects Arthur to smile or laugh, neither of which Arthur does. Scrappy says, "Mother read a bunch of Shakespeare. Bet you can figure which book she finished just before I was born. Coulda been worse. Coulda been Brutus."

Arthur steps close to his friend and nods slightly, his face a deadpan.

"Julius. You don't say." Then he reaches out a hand and claps his friend on the shoulder and says, "Scrappy suits you better."

What tension Scrappy Burroughs feels mostly lifts and floats away, a shoulder-sagging burden swept to the side of the road, swept into a barrow pit. He smiles a little, grunts, and walks outside. Scrappy crunches through the snow, a lightened man, though only a little. The long walk back for him will be good; he will need it to think about what has just taken place. The hard part is over now. It went okay. Arthur understands, nor, does Scrappy think, was he even surprised. Funny how some things in life are harder than you think and some things are not, and most things are never exactly what you expect. But Arthur understands. It had to be done, that's all. Tough news comes to everyone. It's part of life.

Although he is relieved, so relieved, that Arthur understands and their friendship is intact, one gnawing thought rattles in his head: Scrappy struggles with the fact that he has let down a friend, his fault or not.

And for Scrappy Burroughs, there is no worse way to feel.

Chapter Thirteen

WINTER TURNS ITS HEAD AWAY in February then blinks and yawns and grows tired. A corner has been turned. The cold breaks, the clouds become puffy and white, not the blank, gray snow-bearing variety. When it rains, it is a spring shower, not cold winter moisture. Snow melts; the exposed soil is black, rich, wet, and musty. Daylight stretches, the sun takes on a higher slant in the southern sky. Creeks begin to fill with run-off. On his long walks, seeking piecework, or just seeking peace, Arthur notices the first few sparrows and wrens in flitting dance and flight.

At the schoolhouse, Daniel and Anne Durham notice the change and their worries ease. There will be no more punishing winds and driving snowstorms, they conclude; there will be no need to worry about the children overnighting at school. The pile of blankets and extra clothes can be sent home soon, and the cache of canned goods so carefully gathered and discreetly stored in their home will not be needed, not at least for this year. The Andrews brothers plan for planting their crops; Scrappy Burroughs prepares for a short lambing season, knowing he'll do so without Arthur and the other hired hands he has counted on in the past. Bowker the hermit, grizzled, reeking, flecks of canned fish and wild game tangled in his frizzy beard, emerges from his dugout into the late February sunshine, blinks hard in the blinding, dazzling light—the first venture out since late January. Crocus tips break through the soily crust and begin to push the clods aside. The first snow-drops appear, in timely tandem with winter wolfsbane, followed soon by daffodils and hyacinth. A pleasant sociality revives. Neighborly pilgrimages are made; forgotten winter news revived and exchanged, along with baked bread, canned fruits, put-up preserves and stored-up gossip.

The grandeur of sharing buds and flowers snaps alive as winter wanders away and spring comes home.

The subtle change of the season is not lost upon the plains residents. Winter had come, winter had blown hard, winter had challenged and cajoled and pierced and punished them wherever they were—in their homes, out of their homes, in every way it could—but they had not let it overcome them. Winter had not triumphed. The people and their land had. And with that knowledge, they begin to feel the slightest trace of hope as the signs of spring take tender hold.

It is in this spirit of thaw and triumph, of the harsh test administered and passed, of life and Lazarus restored, that Reverend Ennis Popplestone begins visiting members of his flock on the south side of the river. Reverend Popplestone, spindly, gawky, sandy-haired, long in leg and arm, once read Peter's description of the Lord as a man who simply went about doing good; at a time when Ennis was trying to figure out just what his ministry should be, the apostle's unadorned words made sense to him, and he'd adopted the phrase as his guiding light. All in all, it is not a bad choice as a guiding star. Ennis Popplestone is not a complicated man, nor is his theology deep or vexing. He takes little notice of the wrathful Old Testament God; he has no use for cruelty, punishment, and hellfire, except in the most extreme cases when people certainly deserve a celestial thrashing. Ennis Popplestone is a man of almost no guile, and he simply wants to help others over the rocky roads they travel; to share in their sorrow, lift when they are down, heal when they are ill, and from a suitable distance, share in their joys.

Most of the time, he is almost sure that God exists and has a plan for him and every other of His mortal creations, from people to trees to cattle to mountain lions. The young minister feels it is important for every soul to discover just what the plan is. In his case, the call of a shepherd, of protecting a flock from slavering wolves, of helping people to not only cross stormy waters but occasionally walk upon them, seemed a natural fit. He has a good heart and the desire to help, and those qualities alone seem to qualify him for the ministry. Coupled with his two-year certificate of graduation from a mail-order seminary and a desire to leave his native Iowa for somewhere in the West, Reverend Popplestone's calculus was set. Through the friend of a friend who had a second cousin in Twin Falls, he had learned of a ministerial opportunity for a small congregation in Idaho; a letter of introduction accompanied by a facsimile of his theological certificate, and the congregation of farmers and ranchers, all of whom knew far more than he did about herding sheep, had become his to lead in all things spiritual.

On a cold but sunshine-drenched Saturday, Reverend Popplestone, all thrashing legs and arms and with a determination to make someone's load lighter, strides to the porch of Arthur Bell's home and raps on the door, the cold stinging and sizzling his knuckles.

Mary spies him on the porch and is horrified. Lucas, Samuel, and Mercy May sit at the kitchen table with a deck of cards playing hearts. Mary makes a swift, terrible decision. It will not do for a preacher to enter her home and see three children playing with face cards. What would he think? That she and Arthur allowed vice to flourish in their home? Word could spread quickly among the other homes on the plain. It would only take an idle comment to Mrs. Frankie Gabbert or Mrs. Dorothy Harris and the tale of cards and who-knows-what-other-kinds-of-sin would spread as quickly as a down-canyon breeze from the Jarbidge Mountains in August.

She acts with swiftness and surety. She scoops the cards from the table as her stunned children watch and dispatches them into the fireplace. Playing cards. They are not cheap. They cost a quarter a deck. During the icy winter nights, when there was little else to do, the cards—these instruments of Lucifer—were the family's salvation. And now, gone, as the flames first lick and then consume them in the orange-and-purple fire. The three children stare. Mary turns back to them and says with quiet resolve, "Reverend Popplestone is on our porch. You will sit while we visit, and you will behave. There will be no mention while he is here of the cards or anything else that is unseemly or improper that might occur in this house."

And with that, she invites him in.

"Good morning, Reverend."

"Good morning, Mrs. Bell."

"Come in and sit down, please. May I get you something warm to drink? Take the chill out of you. It's still awfully cold."

"No, thanks, Mrs. Bell. I've been to other homes this morning and taken coffee and tea. Any more and I would likely float back to the church."

At this, he winces. Even the vaguest references to bodily functions is not the bearing of a man of God. But to his relief, Mary Bell, nor her children, seem to take much notice, although the little girl—her name? Martha, Mabel, Maddy, something with an *M*—seems to be suppressing a giggle.

Mary says, "My husband and two of our boys are out scavenging some lumber. An old barn over toward Rock Creek was set to tip over. So the owner—Golden Driggs, I believe is his name—said it was wide open for anyone to take. Some of the lumber is good enough to build with, I heard. The other, we'll just burn. We plan to make an addition to our home, a room for our Mercy May, made of stone and scrap lumber. She's the only girl, and it won't do to have her in the same room with the boys. It took some convincing for my husband, but he now sees it is important."

Ennis Popplestone looks around the home and silently assesses: simple, clean, nothing fancy. People here are probably struggling for money. A good fire, though with odd-colored flames, orange and blue more than yellow.

An awkward hush settles in the Bell home. Truth be told, Ennis Popplestone is not well-suited to making small talk. He sometimes feels as though there is nothing in his head—no observation, no thought, no emotion to express. Gabbiness and glibness will never be part of his ministerial repertoire. For a preacher, it presents a considerable conundrum.

He recalls a passage from one of his church-school texts: "When meeting congregants for the first time, or when the congregants are not well-known to the Ordained, it is advisable to initiate and urge on conversation so as to alleviate worry and discomfit. Several topics are of universal interest to people of all walks of life, including the news, the health of their family, or the weather. Politics, sporting ventures, crops, and fey conversation about others ought to be avoided, especially politics, as some of your pastoral flock may be Democrats or Bolsheviks, unbeknownst to you."

The recollection of the passage is a relief, a life preserver tossed into stormy waters. He steers toward safe territory and says somberly, "Long winter we've had, Mrs. Bell."

Mary smiles demurely. "Yes, indeed. There still might be some to go yet. We've been here long enough to know you can count on a false spring or two every year."

On the old couch, sitting between her brothers, Mercy May squirms and wonders why adults always talk about the weather. She smugs up her nose and rolls her eyes. She is bored and her cards burned. It is not a good day for her. She itches to take matters into her own hands.

The young preacher stretches his long thin legs and folds one over the other. Clearly, the analysis of the weather is over.

He grasps again, feeling for another safe topic.

"Your family, Mrs. Bell. Tell me about your family."

Mary says, "There's Arthur and me, who you know, and the three you see sitting here. Then there's Silas and James Richard, out with their father. That's our clan. Arthur isn't one for much religion, although he believes and we say grace at supper and most time at breakfast. But he seems more religious when he has good soil, good seed, good weather, and plenty of water. He knows something's up with this life but hasn't quite figured it all out yet. I thought you should know."

"Thank you, Mrs. Bell. I think we're all religious in some way but just have different means of showing it."

Reverend Popplestone then plays a card of his own, in a manner of speaking. He says to Mercy May, "You're the only girl here besides your mother. You must be spoiled some, what with all these big brothers around."

If it were a card game, the reverend just drew a two of clubs.

Mercy May glowers at the preacher. "I'm not spoilt at all. I work just like my brothers. And we don't have enough to spoil anyone around here."

Mary wishes that face cards were her only trouble at the moment. She gives a look to Mercy May that says, *Enough, young lady. I will deal with you later.* Trying to salvage the situation, she placidly looks at Ennis Popplestone and says, "Mercy May is our little crackerjack. She's awfully smart, and she loves poetry. She does real good at school. Can you recite part of a poem for Reverend Popplestone? I'm sure he would like to hear something you know by heart."

Mercy May, smarting from the glance and rebuke of her mother and still unhappy about the loss of the playing cards on account of the lanky young preacher's unannounced appearance at the Bell family's doorstep, rises from the old creaky couch, stands primly, and begins to recite a poem freshly committed to memory.

> *Whenever Richard Cory went down town,*
> *We people on the pavement looked at him:*
> *He was a gentleman from sole to crown,*
> *Clean favored, and imperially slim.*

Mary sits back, her shoulders slump, and a small smile passes across her face. Her pride in her only daughter flushes away the cold Saturday-morning air. And what a poem! Richard Cory, a good man, clean-favored, and imperially slim. After five children, imperially slim is not in her life's equation, but clean-favored is. She glances at her home, the three children present. Tidy, neat, organized. Perhaps clean-favored could describe the Bell house and its denizens.

Clearly she is not familiar with the poem "Richard Cory."

Mercy May continues, her voice little-girl velvet.

> *And he was always quietly arrayed,*
> *And he was always human when he talked,*
> *But still he fluttered pulses when he said,*
> *"Good morning," and he glittered when he walked.*

A very good poem to recite, Mary thinks. Her daughter is redeeming herself, somewhat. She envisions a man who glitters when he walks. A gentleman. Truly.

Mercy May continues through the next stanza about how everyone wishes they were in Richard Cory's place and then recites the final lines. Mercy May continues, politely, sweetly, angelically. Mary, a woman not given to pride in any form, in this moment, though, wishes an audience—a big, adoring throng, to listen to her precocious daughter repeat the words of this beautiful poem about this wonderful man, the well-favored and imperially slim Richard Cory.

So on we worked, and waited for the light,
And went without the meat and cursed the bread;
And Richard Cory, one calm summer night,

And here Mercy May makes what can only be described as a devilish face, lowers her voice, clenches her teeth, and growls,

Went home and put a bullet through his head.

Mercy May's features change again to sunshine and lightness, she smiles charmingly, does a little curtsy, and plops down on the couch between her gaping brothers.

And for years in the family, the debate rages on. Did Mercy May know what she was doing? Did she select that poem with a purpose, to gain a measure of comeuppance against Ennis Popplestone, the man responsible for the cards being thrust into the fire and who hinted that she might be spoiled? Or was it all innocent happenstance?

Mercy May, for her part, always claims the latter. "A good poem with a punch line," she explains. Mrs. Durham had introduced it to the class only the week before. But as she proclaims her innocence, there is always a glimmer of a smile, a hint of mirth adorning her eyes.

Mary sits stunned. Richard Cory was not who she thought he was. Clean-favored. Imperially slim. Admirably schooled in every grace. Bah! She is betrayed by the gentleman Richard Cory. If only Arthur were here. He, with his liking of poetry, would have known that Richard Cory was a fraud, a sham, and would have stepped in and steered the recitation away from the precipice of disaster. And her daughter. Her daughter—why, oh why, with the preacher sitting in the room would she pick *that* poem? Humiliated beyond expression! Her sons might have just as well pulled out a flask of whiskey and offered a snort to the reverend. She wishes for a yawning Old Testament crater to open up and welcome her into it and then to close over quietly, quickly. The cards seem a trifle now in the spiritual hierarchy of all wickedness.

And Reverend Popplestone.

He sits quietly for a moment, only a heartbeat or two. He sees Mary's keen embarrassment, her clear perturbation. He sees the wide-eyed brothers. He sees Mercy May, undeniably proud of herself and undeniably spoiled. What to make of this? There is no passage from a text to guide his actions, no quick homily to turn water to wine, to feed the five thousand, to transform chagrin to comfort.

So he does what is natural to him. He does what he will do thousands more times in his ministry in years ahead. He does what will make him known and beloved to his small congregation along the plain now and, in the future, to other worshippers in grander settings.

He simply lets his humanity take over.

He smiles. He giggles. He laughs. He guffaws, he chortles, he chuckles. A deep, soul-cleansing, mind-clearing, honest bellow, a blast of laughter. And in that moment, Reverend Popplestone produces the first miracle of his ministry. Not a huge miracle as miracles go, but one that he will look back on in years to come and remember. It was the first time he may have changed a human heart: Mary's.

Mary begins to smile, and it is infectious. Mercy May, Lucas, and Samuel soon join in, a joyous cavalcade of noise floating from the small Bell home. Their laughter far exceeds the humor of the situation, but once that kind of laughter starts, it is impossible to press the brakes to it until all the tears are gone and there simply is no more energy left.

When that moment comes, Reverend Popplestone, weak and wheezy from the sheer joy of it all, wanly asks, "Mrs. Bell, I need you and your children and your husband to stop by church, if only occasionally. You are the kind of people who can make others forget their troubles, and the Almighty Himself knows we need your kind in this day. Sunday School starts promptly at ten."

And how can Mary say no? It is the day, the hour, the precise moment that the Bell family gets beyond tepid, go-through-the-motion religion. All started by grating verse and the unchecked peals of laughter that followed. The next day, she, Mercy May, Lucas, Samuel, Silas, and James Richard bundle up and take the wagon to the small church with the big steeple up toward Filer. Arthur promises he'll come someday, but his conversion wiggles and waggles and never runs in a straight-line course toward heaven's gate, other than the fact that he is a plain good man, which still counts for much.

And from the experience, Reverend Popplestone grows in wisdom and stature. He finds, more firmly than before, that he and God agree on most things, and certainly the most important things. He is a man who learns to never miss the

meaning behind an experience, good or bad, mundane or profound. He comes
to believe, in fact, that God has sent his children to earth, in good measure, to
have as many experiences as they can and learn from them; Reverend Popplestone
thinks all of God's children will be better able to serve as angels in the afterlife
if they only remember what they learned in their earthly existence and put it to
good use.

He rarely again starts a conversation with the unconverted or skeptics by
speaking of the weather.

And as time wears on and he gets to know his little flock better, he also realizes that among them are more than a few Democrats and at least a couple of
Bolsheviks.

And he quickly learns to love them all.

Chapter Fourteen

THE SEALED ENVELOPE CONTAINS A letter, a cryptic letter from Anne Durham to Mary and Arthur. In a flowing, flowery, cursive style—*Easterner's hand. Finishing school*, thinks Mary—the schoolteacher asks if she could come by the Bell home Thursday next and talk about Mercy May for a few minutes. *It is a meeting of some importance*, Anne Durham notes in the letter, *and requires attention. Not urgent*, she writes, but based on her observation of Mercy May, a decision is forthcoming. *And it would be best if Mercy May is not in the house when the visit is made.*

Mary thinks, *Oh, she's surely pulled some stunt and the teacher wants to talk about it. After what she did with Reverend Popplestone here, I can only imagine what is going on at school.*

She confers with Arthur that evening. Arthur studies the letter at the worn kitchen table, turns his head to one side and then another, allows his mouth to droop, and scratches his head. "I don't expect it's nothing of much importance. She doesn't raise any alarms or say it has to do with Mercy May's behavior. Maybe she wants to put on a play or poem recital of some sort, or maybe it's that she's not getting along with some other kid. Yes, we need to have her stop by and hear what she has to say," Arthur concludes. "We don't have much choice."

On the appointed late afternoon, Arthur asks Mercy May and Lucas to take the wagon back toward Rock Creek and pick up more scrap lumber from a fallen barn for possible use in the long-anticipated addition to the home. Mercy May and Lucas leap at the chance to take the family's old gelding horse, Jenks, and the creaky flat-bellied wagon on an important excursion, a rare treat and a vote of confidence from their father. They know he is fussy about just who gets to use that wagon and where it will be pulled.

So they start out on their way in high spirits. The sun stays up until a little after six; by this time, they should be home in time for supper.

Anne Durham putters up to the Bell home not twenty minutes after Lucas and Mercy May start the errand. She drives a Buick, new to the Durhams, purchased from a man named Lind in Twin Falls. The Durhams cannot afford such a luxury on the eighty dollars a month they're each paid, but Anne hails from a wealthy family, and during a conversation over Christmas, her father discerns that a transportation system better than foot, horse, and dependence on others is needed by his daughter and, like most fathers, he is happy to indulge her, and he mails her a check with strict orders to purchase a car for safety and convenience, and he also sternly counsels her to buy from General Motors.

The automobile is a shiny status symbol on the plain, and Anne and Daniel take pride in driving it around. A 1932 Buick, six-cylinder, four-door, ninety-eight-horsepower engine. Boxy through the body and boxy on top but stylish; swan's neck curves on the fenders and wheel wells. It is quite the car, a trophy, in the west end of the Magic Valley. The Durhams know it and are decent enough to be slightly ashamed of it. To even things up a bit, to show that the Pennsylvania-bred schoolteachers have no airs, they solemnly covenant to allow others to use it when the need arises because their friends and acquaintances have been so convivial about taking them to and fro when walking would not have been convenient, and in some cases, even wise, given the rough winter weather and long overland distances. The Andrews brothers, in particular, have made themselves available upon the waggle of a finger; they have shown up at the small schoolhouse on horse, with a wagon, or in their old pickup truck and offered their taxiing services for no more than a smile from Anne Durham or a bit of talk from Daniel about what it is like to sit in Forbes Field and watch Honus Wagner play for the Pittsburgh Pirates.

"We'll just let it be known this car belongs to many people in this community," Daniel says, and it's just not talk. He means it. And he keeps his word. "Free to us, and free to them."

Anne steps lightly out of the car and smooths the creases in her blue wool coat. She adjusts her hat and walks with a purpose to the Bell's front door. She looks at the plain, small Bell home and thinks, *I hope what I am about to suggest is right. I think it is. I hope they will understand. I don't know if this is right after all, but I think it is.*

Anne Durham is already developing an educator's instinct about children and learning and possibilities far beyond her edge of the Magic Valley. She, at times, sees much more in the ragged children than do their own parents. And she already loves them almost as much.

She taps on the door, and Arthur shivers with a quick doubt and thinks, *I hope Mercy May hasn't been scrapping with the Jensen boy anymore,* and he and Mary greet her warmly. It is the first time Arthur has met Anne Durham, and he is impressed by her bearing—tall, robust, and dignified, clear-eyed, someone who seems to soak up each detail and understands nuance. And she drives a Buick. A new, glinty Buick, something not seen often in this part of the plain. Arthur concedes she is a woman of strength and substance and may have things to say of gravity and import. He will listen to her with an open mind.

He beckons her to the couch while he and Mary pull up scratched and slightly wobbly kitchen chairs.

"May I get you something to drink, Mrs. Durham?"

"Tea would be lovely, but only if it would not be too much work," Anne says, and Mary rises from her chair after having been seated for only a few seconds and walks to the kitchen and begins the business of making a small pot of Earl Grey for her visitor.

It takes only a moment for Anne Durham to reveal the purpose of her visit. *Direct, no dancing around,* thinks Arthur, and the young schoolteacher notches another point in favor with him because he believes honesty and straightforwardness are close cousins and fair relatives.

And yes, Mary's and Arthur's intuition was true. The conversation will be about Mercy May. It has nothing to do with her tempestuous relationship with young George Jensen, who, even at this tender age, dreams at night of the day when he can make Mercy May his wife. It will not be about James Richard, a sweet and docile youngster, a pleaser by nature.

Anne Durham says, "James Richard and Mercy May are in my class, as I am sure you know. James Richard is a fine student, companionable in every way, well-liked by his fellow students. It is Mercy May of whom I wish to speak to you in specifics. She is a delight to have and has in some ways made my first year teaching memorable. As I am sure you know, she is exceptionally bright, perhaps even gifted in some ways."

"We had that figured," says Arthur, who dwells for a moment on the word "gifted," a word he likes very much. "She reads so much. Some fine magazines, the *Saturday Evening Post* and *Coronet* and such. They're sent to us by my older sister, Mrs. Lollie Vanoy, from Tennessee, where she is well-to-do on account of her husband being the postmaster. Mercy May snatches those magazines as fast as they come in and reads every one of them, cover front to cover back, advertisements included."

Mary hands a cup of hot tea to Anne Durham and joins the chorus of praise. "Mercy May was reading a long time before she went to school. She *is* a bright one. She and her daddy read often poetry to each other in the evenings."

The parents both ease a bit in their thinking. The meeting with Mrs. Anne Durham was not to be a disciplinary hearing at all. No punishments will be spoken of, no penance meted out.

Anne Durham says some more. "Yes, I noticed her affinity for poetry. I honestly believe that for some poems, she can read through them once and then recite them from memory. She did that just last week, with a poem by Mr. E. A. Robinson called, 'Richard Cory.' Your daughter has a wonderful mind."

Mary suppresses a grimace and remains outwardly placid at the mention of the disgraced gentleman Richard Cory and only adds, "Yes, we've all become familiar with that poem of late. A sad ending, though, to the life of a fine gentleman."

Anne Durham remains on task. "It's because of her scholastic aptitude that I would like you to think about a decision that we'll be facing in the next few months. The decision is this: I believe Mercy May will benefit by skipping a grade, and perhaps even two, at the end of the school year. I believe that she will only be held back by what I teach in the third grade and that her learning will accelerate and she will be challenged more and therefore be less restricted and disengaged if we advance her curriculum next fall. At this point, it's only a thought and a suggestion, but it is something all of us need to keep in mind. You as her parents will have the final say, of course."

Arthur and Mary react as any parents would: They beam. They nod. They feel the swell of excitement, the pride of those who see their children do well.

Mrs. Anne Durham, though, is not finished.

"I didn't know what to expect when I came to Idaho to teach. I didn't know if the children would be ready to learn or even if they would want to learn. I fervently hoped that I would find, somewhere on this plain, a student who is gifted. I believe that is the case with your daughter."

Arthur and Mary, unused to any shower of praise, only look at each other and smile awkwardly, embarrassed in the sunlight of praise. Then Arthur reaches across and shyly takes Mary by the hand. This girl of his, he thinks amiably, has turned out real well.

"She must attend high school," Mrs. Anne Durham says. "That's a given. It would be a miscarriage of fairness and a waste of a fine intellect were she to withdraw from further schooling after the eighth grade. And then she must consider college. She would, I believe, excel at the university level."

College! For Arthur and Mary, the suggestion might as well have been to send their youngest child to Jupiter and back. It was never considered, a topic that never surfaced in the waves of conversation. Never. Incomprehensible. Something for other people, wealthy people, people with more opportunity and people with more privilege. Their own child?

And with those few words, Mrs. Anne Durham, who came all the way to Idaho from Pennsylvania to teach, to open possibilities and unlock dreams, has succeeded—not with a child, in this case, but with the parents of a child.

"It needs to be our long goal," she says to the now near-mute Arthur and Mary. "You're worried about money, but there are ways around the financial obligations. Yet as I said, all of that is for days to come. For the remainder of the school year, I wish to put Mercy May on an accelerated scholastic program. I would like to give her more homework, challenge her mind more than I have up to this point. With your permission, I occasionally would like to take her to Buhl and perhaps Twin Falls on Saturdays to the library."

Mary is stunned to hear of the field trips to the library. To this point in her life, she has always assumed that libraries—stiff, tall, granite-columned—required a fee to enter. Libraries were for people of means. She remains silent but is gratified that her daughter would soon become familiar with a place that until that moment seemed faraway, forbidden, and foreboding.

"Your daughter may come home cross with me at times, but I hope you will support my endeavors with her. My only goal is to further train her beautiful mind and prepare her for a better education and therefore a better life."

Arthur and Mary sit in shocked silence. They manage a nod and mumble their approval of the plan and thank the stately young schoolteacher for her interest in their daughter. The conversation about Mercy May winds down at that point. The dream seed has been planted with Arthur and Mary. Mrs. Anne Durham sips her tea politely and begins talking about prices and crops and how long the winter has lasted. She has assimilated to many of the ways and topics of people who live on the Snake River Plain, this woman who, upon her arrival a mere seven months ago, would have bolted for Pennsylvania with the slightest of nudges from her husband. When the teacup is empty, she stands and excuses herself. Arthur rises and walks her to the door. Daylight is ebbing; the sun is being overtaken by high cirrus clouds and farther to the west, a bruised ocean-sky of purple and gray is rolling toward the Bell home. But in the numbing afterglow of the conversation with the teacher, none of them notice the ominous change in the weather blowing up from Glenns Ferry.

Mrs. Anne Durham catches Arthur's lustful look at the Buick and, remembering the promise she'd made with Daniel, offers, "Would you like to take the automobile on a quick drive, Mr. Bell? You'll find she handles decently and provides a comfortable ride. I can stay here with Mrs. Bell for a few minutes and get caught up on some other things."

Arthur is tempted. It would be the finest automobile he has ever been in, much less driven. He is a man who relies on his lumber wagon and two horses for transportation. A Buick. A shiny black Buick with big curved fenders over the front and back wheels. Finally, he says shyly, "If you wouldn't mind. I will make it quick. I can be back in five minutes."

"Take your time, Mr. Bell. I want to talk with your wife a little more about James Richard. He's a very bright youngster."

And off he trots toward the car before she takes back her promise—though she doesn't seem to be the kind to do that—or adds restrictions. Couldn't blame her for that.

Driving it up the road, turning off toward town, running it at a brisk pace in front of Mr. Sperry's store and at least one saloon, it is one of the few times in Arthur Bell's life when his word and deed did not form an exact square. It was forty-five minutes later when he returned, dark outside, and the dark boiling lapis cloud had settled on the plain, smothering the land in its icy grasp.

"She runs real fine," Arthur says sheepishly. "I got carried away a bit and drove her farther than I expected. You could lose yourself driving an automobile like that."

Mary is grateful he is back, but she has been looking outside for the last half hour and wondering where Lucas and Mercy May are and how they are doing and if the dark fog bank would find them, overtake them, cause them to spin in confusion, shiver from cold and fear, and get lost. Mary paces in front of the house, worry descending on her like a shroud.

The children are overdue.

***

Lucas and Mercy May pick over the salvage lumber from the tumbledown barn. There isn't much left of it, only a few boards that can be used for Mercy May's new room. The thrill of being asked to take on an assignment of responsibility quickly wears off. Now comes the work, sorting through the broken boards, watching out for nails, looking for any piece good enough to build with or bad enough to burn. Mercy May is especially scrupulous; she examines each piece of barn wood and tries to image it as part of the wall of her new room.

They keep at the work, heads down, and don't notice the purple-and-gray curtain of ice fog churning toward them.

By dusk, the cloud bank rolls over them, smothering the land, seeming to snuff out the very life of anything that walked, crawled, scuttled, or breathed. The temperature drops twenty degrees in minutes. Icy flakes glitter and swirl and settle on anything stationary; frozen jewelry on trunk, stem, branch, and twig. In the space of a half hour, the complexion of the day changes completely. Winter, on a solo final fling, comes back in a way both soft and violent; it blows a velvety icy fog onto the plain and deep into the valley.

"We'd better get out of here," Lucas says. "We can come back another time for the rest of the scrap."

Mercy May needs no further encouragement and scrambles onto the wagon.

Lucas turns the wagon around on the road, and they plunge deeper into the evening's icy veil. Light is shriveling and dying.

At the Bell home, Mary looks outside into the gloom. Anne Durham left twenty minutes ago, just ahead of the gaping maw of the silent storm.

"Will they be okay, Arthur? It looks terrible outside. They're awfully young to be out in an ice fog like this."

With more calm than he feels, Arthur says, "They should be fine, Mary. Ol' Jenks can find his way home through anything. Lucas will think his way through it. If Lucas is smart, he'll just let the horse have its way and they'll be home in no time."

Nevertheless, he tilts his head and nods at Samuel, Silas, and James Richard, his signal that it's time to organize a search party. With no rattle in his voice or hike in volume, he says to Mary that he and the boys will go out and walk down the road a piece just to make sure Lucas and Mercy May get home. The boys bundle up, grab a couple of lanterns from the barn, and follow their father down the road.

On the wagon, the fog envelopes and tugs at Lucas and Mercy May. She shivers and slides closer to her brother. She grabs his arm and puts her head on his shoulder.

"Will we be okay? Are we lost?"

Lucas looks ahead, into the darkness. He can see no more than twenty feet. Landmarks have disappeared in the black soup. He has lost the road. They are traveling overland. He doesn't know if he is headed north, south, east, or west. He could be dangling at the edge of Rock Creek Canyon. Or he could be on the plain and only yards from home. He holds the reins loosely in his hands, allowing Jenks to find the road and get them home.

"I wouldn't say we're lost," Lucas says. "Because I know about where we are. It's just the 'about' part that has me a little curious."

He tries not to worry, tries not to panic. He justifies the faith of his father and tries to think through the predicament. Jenks slows. The cold starts to bite, the ice in the air needles into their lungs. They take quick, shallow breaths. Mercy May's fingers and toes tingle and sting. She has no feeling in her face, and speech becomes difficult, an effort to just form words and spit them into the black air.

Lucas thinks, *Dad will come out. My brothers will be with him. They will find us and take us home.*

He says as much to Mercy May, who brightens at the thought. Then she puts her head back on her brother's shoulder and seems to fall asleep.

Slow, slow. Everything is slow and cold.

Lucas thinks some more. If no one finds them, what should he do? He thinks they should crawl into the back of the wagon and huddle for warmth and avoid the slap of the fog and ice and trifle of a breeze. He could pull the scrap lumber over them, though he knows that will do little to keep them warm, but he understands the appearance of doing something is almost the same as doing something in the eyes of his sister.

Or should he just start walking, trying to find a gentle, pale light spilling from a home? Should he leave his sister here while he seeks help from somewhere else? *No.* The word bursts its way into his tottering consciousness. He cannot leave Mercy May to the cruel invasion of ice and fog and bitter cold. He would perish with her rather than leave her.

He has no matches. Matches. What he would give for a single match. He could start a fire, which would provide warmth and act as a signal to anyone who would be searching for them. He will never, he decides, leave his home again, when the weather may turn foul, without matches in his pocket.

Jenks stops. He just stops. He will not take another step into the chilled inky darkness. Lucas prods and urges and even curses at the animal, but Jenks will not take another step. The horse is lost too, Lucas reluctantly concludes.

The feeling in Lucas's feet, legs, arms, hands, and face disappears. A chill with the vehemence of an earthquake runs the length of his body. Mercy May still seems to sleep. He feels her shudder violently.

"Mercy May, come on! We've got to get up!" He rustles her shoulder and pats her cheeks. He takes her hands into his and rubs them and blows his breath on them.

She moves, and then in a voice slow, deep, and clumsy, she asks, "Are we home?"

"Not yet, but we're close. It's just up ahead a little. Jenks has stopped, so we'll have to walk the rest of the way. We'll be in front of the fireplace in five minutes."

"I don't want to go. I don't want to walk. I'll just stay here. You can go get Daddy, and he'll come and get me and bring me home," she mumbles thickly.

"No, we need to go now. We need to walk," Lucas pleads.

"I don't want to."

And with that, she sleeps again.

Lucas climbs off the wagon, making sure Mercy May doesn't fall sideways off the seat. He pulls her toward him and wraps his arms around her back. Her head rests again on one of his shoulders. She maunders something he can't understand. He cinches her higher, and her legs rest on his hips. And then he starts walking, stumbling, tripping into the night.

Two hours have passed since the frigid fog rolled through and swamped the plain.

The fog encrusts him in icy crystals. His breath comes in short bursts. The freezing, fizzy, damp air seems to shred his lungs with each breath.

He must sit down. For a moment. Not long. His mind is dense and slow, and his thoughts come as though he were walking in knee-high mud. He will sit down. Then he will get up and carry his sister home. But a minute. Just to rest. He is so very weary.

And Lucas sits down and leans up against a large sagebrush and closes his eyes.

The night, the darkness, the cold, the ice, the fog suffocates all living things, relentlessly covering the tops of trees, working its way between the blades of grass, and fingering its way under the brush. No place is left untouched. Winter sends a final, chattering call across the Snake River Plain.

Lucas doesn't know how long he sleeps, but it is a dizzying, shuddery, and dream-filled slumber, the icy cold creeping in from his edges, paralyzing his feet and hands, thickening his thoughts. And then he senses someone or something nearby, hears the crunching noise of animal movement. He is not afraid. He is too cold to be afraid. He only wants the nightmare to end. He feels a hand on his shoulder. A whiff of something musky and ripened, the faint odor of whiskey followed by stale, sour, hot breath, and he opens his eyes.

A face.

A spectral, wooly face is bent over him, a gloriously whiskery, grimy, grinning, homely face.

And he hears a whistle. A four-note, high-pitched whistle that seems to ask, "Are you okay?"

Praise be to heaven.

Mr. Bowker is out wandering tonight.

***

The searchers have been away for almost an hour. Word along the plain spreads quickly: two of Arthur and Mary Bell's children got caught in the late-winter ice fog and are missing. The men come, some on horses, others in their trucks, some with lanterns, others with flashlights. Scrappy Burroughs and his sons are the first at the Bell home, followed quickly by the Andrews brothers, Ken Bailey, Amos Hamilton, Ennis Popplestone, skinny Frank Kowlaski, hot-tempered Squat Perkins, plus a dozen more. Jo Powell drives her flatbed truck into the yard. Arthur and his three other sons had had no luck finding the children. The search now will expand. Arthur, Scrappy, and Jo draw on a big sheet of paper the grid that each team of two searchers will cover. Their breath comes in billowy steam, pale vapors against the silver-blackness of the fog bank.

Arthur tells everyone of his gratitude that they'd come out on a miserable night such as it is. He asks them to be careful themselves, for on a night like this, even the most experienced man or woman could wind up turned around and in trouble. Arthur stands aside and lets Scrappy take over. Arthur's insides are churning, and his breast feels as though it is weighted by stone, and he knows he cannot be counted on for right thinking. Scrappy clears his throat and coughs and says they all know what the outcome might be and, by thunder, he wouldn't stand for anything other than the two children to be safe and warm in their own beds that very night. He tells everyone to come back and check in at ten o'clock, and if no progress is made, they'd regroup and search some more, all night if needed. Scrappy calls everyone together for their assignments. Then, with only a few words and nods, they spread out. Ennis Popplestone suggests prayer, and all in the assembly lower their chins and after the entreaty, mumble, "Amen."

They are men who face long odds with nothing more than a bob of the head, a big-pawed hand on Arthur's shoulder, and a few words of encouragement. They are calm and practical as they begin the hard business of the night.

Nobody says it aloud, but everyone at the Bell's place knows it and thinks it: if the two children aren't found soon after midnight, they may not be found alive by morning.

They disperse into the dark on a mission, cobbled of part hope and part horror, bound in gritty determination. Light from the swaying lanterns they carry is gobbled up in the shrouded cold night within two dozen yards of the Bell home.

***

Mary stands at the one decent-sized window of her house, staring into the blackness. The searchers have been gone an hour, maybe a little more. She is sick with despair, and her heart seems to seize up as she stares into the impenetrable shield of night. This land. Such a hard, hard land, created to proffer so little forgiveness. She hears something, or so she thinks. Then the sound disappears, smothered by the freezing fog. She closes her eyes in hopes of picking up the sound again, what she believes is the sound of a man's boots scraping along the road. Could it be

Lucas? There is no sound; then there is. She strains. Faint. A distant boot on frozen ground crackling. She waits; she opens her eyes. Out of the dimness she senses shimmering movement. The sound stays this time. Then another sound comes—a dry, reedy whistling. The ghostly motion takes shape. It is a man, beastly in form, with a child carried on his back and his hand extended to a boy, who stumbles along toward the front porch.

Mary steps outside and meets them. She is a woman given to serenity, deliberate in manner, outbursts of emotions as rare as valley snow in August. Yet she feels her heart thumping and banging around inside her chest, and she wants to shout for joy, but with great will, she holds it in. It is not the way of greeting the humpy-backed, broken man slowly taking form in the night.

Reaching the porch, Frederic Bowker nudges Lucas toward Mary. He carefully reaches around and gently lifts Mercy May from his back and into the arms of her mother.

Mary collects herself, fights the tidal wave of emotion, and mildly says to Bowker, as though addressing a sparrow with a broken wing, "Good evening, Mr. Bowker. Thank you for bringing my children home. Arthur will be so relieved, as I am. Would you like to step in and warm yourself up? I could make you some coffee or tea. I have bread, too."

Bowker grins then whistles two low uneven notes that she takes to mean, *No thanks,* and then he turns away and walks back into the darkness, a place of comfort to him.

He reaches his shambled house near the west wall of Rock Creek Canyon well after midnight and wonders if he has done some good on behalf of the family of man, and can't come to a satisfactory answer, because he has too much to make up in life. He stretches, he yawns, he gets a whiff of his own stale smell, which is a comfort to him because it proves he is alive and has not dreamed all this, then he lies prone on the hard slat of a bed and sleeps again within the earth.

***

"Mr. Bowker was a hero," I say to her. "He saved you and Uncle Lucas and returned the tractor to Mr. Burroughs."

Mother nods slowly. "He . . . was. That . . . he was," she says in bumpy rhythm.

We are back at the resort. The television set drones in the background—a game show, silly people jumping up and down and shouting stupid words. Neither of us pay attention.

"We tried to thank him in a more formal way," she says slowly, as though picking her way across a creek, eyeing words as stones and hopping carefully from one to the next. "Daddy managed to get a turkey, Mother got together some canned goods, and we put up a box of her preserves and fruits. We drove the wagon to his sod house near Rock Creek and tried to . . . get him to come out, but he would not. We only wanted to show our—oh my, what is the word?—gratitude. He never came out. Daddy stopped by . . . a couple of days later. The turkey was gone, but the other food . . . was right where we left it. I'm still not sure Mr. Bowker ever took it in. That was . . . his way. We knew enough to respect it. Two days later, we saw hobos near the tracks eating roasted turkey . . . We think . . . we knew where . . . it came from. Mr. Bowker. He was . . . a curious man, a broken puzzle, but his heart was true."

"Did people understand Mr. Bowker? Did they appreciate him?"

"Not at first. Not for a while. But in the end, he was—oh dear, the word—accepted. We came to love him . . . for his differences, not shun him . . . because of them. It was a great . . . early lesson for me. I know how . . . to accept people."

She is wearing down. It has been a tiring day for her. She picks up a book—books still being among her most frequent and favored company—and laboriously reads a page or two. I sit still and think of the stories she has told me and the richness of her family, the experience of the Great Depression, the closeness of that community on the South Plain, and it causes me to wonder what I have missed, what we have missed in our day and time, when good neighbors are defined by fences and how well they mind their own business. And those people. The patriarchal Scrappy Burroughs. The decorous Jo Powell. The mettlesome Andrews brothers. The perspicacious Durhams. And all the others. They each left their indelible good marks upon my mother and her brothers. They each live on, although in memories scrubbed many times through her generation and now fading. And perhaps the most curious and beloved of them all, the eccentric, heartbroken hermit, Frederic Bowker.

Mother, as if reading my thoughts, puts her book on her lap

"Mr. Bowker, you know—that was not the only time . . . he helped us," she says, halting between every few words. "It wasn't long . . . after we were lost in the ice . . . storm that he came to our aid again. That's when . . . the times were at their worst."

She picks up her book again. A book of poems. *One hundred of the finest English poems ever written*, the cover's subtitle reads. After all these years, she still loves the popular poems. She battles her aphasia; she gives no quarter. She fights the odds; she lashes at the medical facts. She is not ready to give up her precious words, her understanding of what others write, not ready to surrender ideas, both hers and those of other people. Not without a struggle, not without pushing back. When she had the stroke near the dining hall at the resort, the newspaper on her lap was opened to the editorial page. Still interested in ideas, notions, opinions, and words, her precious words. She and her mother thought libraries were for the wealthy. She will surround herself with books until her last breath, even if the words in them are scrambled and as indecipherable to her as hieroglyphics scrawled on a Babylonian tomb wall.

She is thinking of Frederic Bowker. A smile flits across her face. Maybe she recalls the grizzled face, the herky-jerky ride on his back, the crust of dirt mixed with body oils, the odor of a man who may have gone months between baths, the scent of drink, the streaked-brown teeth, the greasy hair, the pocked mind, his grit and glorious grime. And then she recounts the part of Bowker that should be remembered most: his heart.

"Mr. Bowker . . . you know, he was . . ." She stops and scans the room and reaches far back into her mind for the right words, simple words, true words. They come to her. "He was our guardian angel. He was . . . a wonderful and kind man."

Chapter Fifteen

ON A DARK LANDSCAPE IN dark times, where storms howl across the plain and dirt rises in the air and settles twenty miles away; when some families have no firm notion of where their meals will come from by week's end; when people just give up and pack their meager belongings and leave in the thick of the night for somewhere, anywhere, that might be better; when work is scarce and money scarcer and no one who works the land hardly will step into a bank for fear they'll lose even more; when it takes will and courage merely to rise and face what ill wind may blow that day; when all of this happens and hope is slowly squeezed out of man or woman or child like wet cotton cranked through a hand wringer; when all of this and more happens; still, there will still be splotches of light, still be laughter of the heart, still be joyous noise and capering, still be people to lift others up and away from life's burdens, temporary though the respite may be.

There will be crackling, sizzling comets flying across the black canvas of the night. Along the plain, the names of those sparkly comets are Ben and Tom Andrews. The Andrews brothers. The Andrews twins. The Andrews boys. No other twosome, by blood, friendship, or happenstance, are more beloved on the plain than they.

They are broad-shouldered, bull-necked, and strong-armed, yet lean; dark hair, brown-complected from days in the sun. They have big wide-set eyes of a blue-and-steel color; toothy, gappy smiles; and the natural light of mischief in their bearings. They are strong, capable, and greathearted. Wherever Benjamin and Thomas Andrews walk, they are noticed, and not because they are bookends save for Ben's slightly pocked left cheek and Tom's inch-long scar over his right eye, branded by a flighty mare that may have been the only creature on God's earth not overtaken by the Andrews boys' good-natured charm.

That is their gift: People see them and they like them, spot on, firmly, the first time. They trust them. They have good feelings about the two before a word has been spoken to the brothers. Men take note and brazenly imagine something of themselves in the Andrews boys, true or not; women fling skyward phantasmagoric and wistful thoughts about walks down church aisles clad in white and becoming the mother of the Andrews boys' children.

If all that were not enough, the Andrews brothers are also just plain good farmers and seem to be getting by fair enough in these difficult days.

The Andrews twins are on their own in 1933 and have been for eight years. Their mother died in 1919 from tuberculosis; a half dozen years later, their churl of a father, Alton, told them one night at the supper table that he was tired of farming and would be leaving on Saturday next for Salt Lake City, where there was more to see and do, although they need not look for him on the Mormons' Temple Square. His destination was decidedly less holy.

"I want to play cards and drink more than I should and walk away from this no-good life. You boys are old enough and smart enough to take over here." Alton sniffed from behind a big bushy moustache and black curly eyebrows. "I've been to the bank and seen a lawyer, and all the papers are done. You two now own most everything, other than the part of the bank savings I'm taking with me as a stake. I'll drop you a letter and let you know where I settle," he told his startled, gape-mouthed sons. A hollow promise, as most of Alton Andrews's were, since he never got around to letting them know where he settled, if he settled anywhere at all. "Now, clean up the table. When the time comes next week, I'll be leaving on the train. You boys can drop me off at the depot. For now, I'm heading into Twin for something to drink."

And the boys didn't see their father again for years, not until they both were married and had sons and daughters of their own, when a wheezy, yellow-eyed, coppery-green-skinned man showed up one evening at Ben's door and announced he was his father. Ben invited him in for supper, called Tom to come over and meet with the old man, and cleared a bed for him to stay in. Alton Andrews was gone the next morning before sunrise, never seen again by either of his sons.

Obviously, Ben and Tom take after their mother, Sophie, remembered as a vivacious and winsome young woman, someone who still aroused a mite of curiosity among those who thought of her: What did Sophie ever see in nettlesome Alton Andrews? And why would she ever agree to marry and settle with a man so dour, so execrable?

So at the age of seventeen, the brothers became landowners, and responsibility was thrust upon them. Their choices were simple: sell out, hire out, or try to make a go of the farm. They chose the latter path. Older farmers on the plain kept an eye on them, gave gentle pointers and more fatherly advice than Alton ever had, and were rewarded when the boys listened and followed through. Their reputations became set in stone: good boys, smart, quick on the take, hard workers. The advice slowed to a trickle after a couple of years, and Ben and Tom Andrews took their place alongside the most respected and productive farmers on the west end of the plain.

The work was strenuous and exhausting, but no matter the long hours, the bruises, the calluses, the missing fingernails, the banged-up hands and blisters, they remained steady in the eyes of other men, steady being high praise to have heaped upon any son of the land.

And their streak of playfulness and affability, and hard work freely given, never wavered.

It was more than the surreptitious children's gifts at Christmas, the sprint to snow banks and the stifled mad laughter that followed. The Andrews twins were everywhere they were needed. Indeed, they seemed to have an extra sense honed in on helping others at the time help was most deserved and welcomed.

When a horse was skittery and needed gentling, nobody was better than the Andrews twins at calming the beast, not even Squat Perkins.

If a young girl sat lonesome in a corner at a grange dance, one of the Andrews boys could be counted on to amble up and ask for the next number, and then not let her out of sight or sit by herself for the rest of the evening.

If extra hands were needed to get in spuds or sugar beets in the frantic race before the first deep freeze, Ben and Tom often just showed up and went to work.

When a family called it quits and needed help loading a truck or wagon in the middle of the night, Ben and Tom somehow found out and were there to lend stout shoulders and strong hands.

When Nord Hall died in an accident in a cornfield shortly after midday one late August, it was the Andrews boys who carried him into the house; laid him out on the table; and while Ben held the quaking widow until the women, the preacher, and the undertaker showed up, Tom took the children round back and tenderly explained that their daddy had gone away but would still look out for them although he could not be seen. "Those Andrews boys," the old-timers grunted. "They got bottom."

Not that they were saints. On certain Saturday nights, when the work was done, the Andrews boys might have quenched their thirst with drink stronger than ginger ale, and when the hay rake gouged Ben's foot, purple invectives spilled forth not unlike lava flushed from a belching volcano. Good men, the Andrews twins, but saints with a small *s*, and their imperfections only endeared them all the more to their friends. They spent more than an hour or two here and there in the confessional, mule-faced and mumbling to the priest on the other side.

But that streak of playfulness, their unchecked frolicsome nature. Knots tied in bootlaces during conversations at a store. Firecrackers popping on a porch at midnight. A horse magically freed of its harness and bolting away unadorned from a wagon. A small handwritten wood sign posted on the county road in front of a home saying, *Kittens wanted. Will pay top dollar.* Official-looking letters, purportedly from the irrigation district, announcing that water shares had been sold cut-rate to the state of California.

So they were beloved, admired, and on their way to legendary status on the plain. They were getting by and a little more during the time of the Great Depression. Yet, they were missing something in life. They knew it, and they ached to change it.

Call it a feeling. An emotional scratch. A curiosity. A pang. A hankering. A hollow, an open spot, a sore, something unfinished because it had never really begun. Restlessness.

So in tune with one another were they that it seemed as though each could read the other's mind as easily as reading the front headline in the Times Review. And as is the case with some sets of twins, they were in the habit of finishing each other's sentences.

It is one evening in their surprisingly tidy bachelor home, as the end of a glorious spring day drew to a close, that they were thinking, these two, the same thoughts, but not about each other, as it turns out.

"Say. I've wanted to ask you about—" Ben says, sitting at a small table after a wheezy, wispy cough.

"Something. Me too," says Tom, sitting back in a wood chair, staring at the ceiling, watching a cobweb lazily float above.

"Has to do with—"

"Courting and women and such stuff."

"Yes. And such stuff."

"We're old enough. And we're not getting younger," Tom appraises.

"Yes, sure enough, and we have—"

"Money enough for both of us and two more."

"And food enough too. I reckon we have six months, maybe closer to a year of goods stored up."

"No woman would ever—"

"Go hungry here with us. And I understand, from listening to older fellows and just by looking in general, that women—"

"Eat more'n you guess."

"'Specially when they've had a few babies and put on a few years—"

"That's a fact. I've noticed."

Tom's glance drops from the cobweb and toward his brother. "We got the food, we should have good crops; the water's okay this year. Prices are lousy, but—"

"Even if they eat more, say more than you'n me, and even more so it surprises us a lot, we should be—"

"Fine, just fine."

Reverie follows, short-lived, pensive, pregnant. Then Ben asks a delicate question. "Who do you think might go with us somewhere? Who might find us, you know,"—and he hesitates, not wanting to use the word, but finding no other, he splurts it out—"attractive?"

Tom, the younger of the brothers by four minutes, but the more confident of the pair, says, "Lots of women, I'd guess. At least for me. I'm the handsomer of us."

"But we're the same," Ben protests. "We're identical twins. We look like each other. People we've known all our lives call me 'Tom.' Ken Bailey did so the other day."

"Well, suit yourself, then," Tom says. "Whatever you think. But I always have believed I'm a handsomer man than you."

"But we look the same."

"Whatever thought gets you by, Ben. But I am handsomer. No doubt."

The brothers fall silent for a few moments, but the question of "Who?" is rattling about. Finally, Tom says, "I think Naomi Kendricks is a nice enough girl. Pretty, too."

"Yep, she is. And with all them younger brothers and sisters running around the house, she'd probably jump at the chance to go dancing or somewhere else with you. Or me, even though you say you're the handsomer of us."

"How about you, then, Ben?"

Ben squinches up his face and drums his fingers on the table, as though giving the question considerable thought, although it is all a front: he has had a case on Chloe Perkins for years. Worshipped her from afar. Ten miles or so, as a matter of fact, the distance between the Perkins' and Andrews' places.

In this little game of brotherly poker, Ben decides to lay out his cards flat on the table.

"Chloe. Chloe Perkins. I've had my eye on her for a little bit. She's a nice enough girl."

He scrutinizes his brother's face for a reaction, but Tom doesn't flinch. Then he nods slowly, then faster, and finally he breaks into a smile.

"I think you're choosing pretty smart," Tom says. "But there is one problem: Her father. Squat can be ornery. In fact, he is ornery. And he'll cheat you if he can."

"The way of the world," Ben says laconically. "I can deal with him. He's a bit like Dad, and we got along okay, right up to when he left us orphaned."

"Can you go through Squat to get to Chloe? Can you put up with his ways?"

"I think so. I hope so. You know, you get him talking about horses, and he's not a half-bad man. He's got his views, all right, and he'll take something if you're not looking, but we've dealt with worse. And you get him talking about something he likes and he's almost civil."

"Almost."

"So what do you think we ought to do, Ben?"

"I think you need to get up to the table and figure out just how we're going to capture the attention of two young ladies."

With that, Tom crabs to the table where Ben is sitting, and they put their heads down and jabber for an hour. In the end, they have a plan. For two bachelors, mostly unschooled in affairs and matters of the heart, and clearly knowing more about the price of sugar beets than women, it's not a bad plan: borrow a car, because a car will impress the two young ladies, and take them on a picnic out toward Blue Lakes. After that, they suspect, the hard part will be over and the rest of their courtships will flow, just flow, and life will be according to nature's way. *It's not as difficult as most people make it out to be,* they conclude. *Anyone can fall in love. It's easy.*

At the end of the planning session, they both feel satisfied and accomplished and allow themselves a glimpse into the future: young men on the rise, sitting at home on Saturday evenings, watching their wives sew or playing cards or jostling with the children. Oh, yes, there will be children. On that count, the brothers are sure. Lots of them.

"Naomi Kendricks," says Ben to his brother. "Hmmm."

"And you. Chloe Perkins. I shoulda seen it," says Tom to his brother.

They sit in idle and pleasant stupor for a few minutes. Then Tom says, "I've got some firecrackers. It ain't too late, is it?"

Ben smiles and says, "It never is." They grab jackets and head into the night toward the front porch of some unsuspecting and soundly sleeping neighbor, giggling and picking at each other every step of the way.

***

At the schoolhouse and the nearby teachers' home, the Andrews brothers are becoming regulars. It is a mystery to Daniel and Anne Durham, but hardly a day goes by without one or both of the twins showing up and making themselves useful.

"Looks like the roof of the house could stand a patch."

"Your firewood stack is paltry; mind if we drop by a half cord of pine?"

"Let me help with that load of groceries, Mrs. Durham."

"Your automobile is a little dusty. We could get a bucket of water and spritz it right up."

"We've got good bacon from one of our own hogs; okay if we brought some by?"

It is a puzzle to the Durhams. They welcome the attention and the extra help but cannot divine the purpose behind the Andrews boys' unending gallantry.

"You don't suppose one or both of them have become fond of you?" Daniel asks after the Andrews have repaired a fence on the back edge of the schoolyard. "They're young men, of course, and handsome at that. They have their drives, you know."

Anne, a tall, strong, and comely woman, dismisses the notion with a careless hand wave. "No, that can't be it. They're not the type," but she is secretly flattered by the suggestion. "And even if that were true, they would not be so overt about it, offering help to the both of us. And not a hint of flirtatious behavior. They're your friends too, dear Daniel."

"I suppose time will tell. It may just be that they're goodhearted sons of Idaho who have taken pity on hapless easterners. We shall see," Daniel says, with a look both amused and ponderous. "Time will tell. But I do so enjoy being your husband. I would like it to stay that way."

"No need to worry. Remember, we are here only because of our predecessor's dalliances. We shall not follow his detestable example."

***

That very evening, the Andrews brothers appraise the status of their plan.

"I think a little more help, get them to trust us just a little more, and we can ask the question," Ben says with a glint of hopefulness in his voice.

"You're right. And they're both real nice people, and it's been good to get better acquainted," says Tom. "I saw old Sam Meldrum driving around Filer in that car of theirs yesterday, and if they'd loan it to him, they'd loan it to us. Sam can't see twenty feet ahead of his nose."

"Let's go over things again," says Ben. "I think we're getting close."

"Sure thing," says Tom. "Let's."

And the brothers pass the remainder of the day plotting, planning, dreaming.

***

Mercy May and Mary are engaged in serious talk, just the two of them, as long shadows stretch across the Bell's yard and steal onto the front porch steps where they sit. Arthur and his sons have gone up to a small creek that tumbles out of the Jarbidges toward the Snake, where the fishing is preternaturally good—a spot that, in the best tradition of fishermen everywhere, they have kept entirely to themselves. Fish on the supper table comes as a welcome relief to the customary potatoes, peas, and sometimes the thinnest nibble of stringy beef or fatty lamb. Mercy May, never one to care much for fishing, has elected to stay at her mother's side, sizing it up as a providential time to talk about a worry and a nemesis.

"She says I have only one dress for school. She says, 'The Bells are poor, because they only have one daughter and she has only one dress.' I can't say anything back to her, because she's right; I only have the one white dress that I wear every day," Mercy May prattles to her mother.

That is her worry.

She is Donna Rose Plumm, who, even at the age of nine, has shown definite tendencies toward priggishness, bumptiousness, and sanctimony; tendencies that will suit her well later in life, when she becomes the wife of an assistant undertaker in Pocatello, president of the church choir, general baroness of overall community morals, and air raid warden of a section of homes along Bannock Avenue. Donna Rose Plumm has three (!) school dresses, although she has not let it be known that they were sent as hand-me-downs from prosperous cousins in Massachusetts.

She is Mercy May's nemesis. Donna Rose Plumm.

Mary says, "Well, you only have one dress. And what Donna Rose says is true, in one way; we don't have much money. You needn't let it bother you."

"But it's not fair. She's got a wart on her ear, but I don't say anything about that. So far, anyway."

"Let people talk, Mercy May. They only hurt themselves. You'll run into others who have a way of turning good things to ugliness. It's a human trait, I suppose. And please do not bring up the wart on Donna Rose's ear."

"But I wish there was something we could do."

Mary runs the toe of her shoe across the doughy soil at the bottom of the stairs.

"Well, just maybe, there is."

***

Mercy May is determined. She is not one to be trifled with. She is not one to declare war against. Donna Rose Plumm does not realize this, mistaking her rival's diminutive size and her single white dress as weaknesses, marking her as easy prey. She is about to find out otherwise.

On the playground, a game of kick-the-can. Donna Rose Plumm, a stout girl and a fast runner, pumps her legs up and down, a smug smile on her face, the can just ahead, victory only yards away. To her left, George Jensen cuts at an angle toward the same can, a gleam in his eyes. There is an intersection of the two, and down they go. In a staggering, scraggly attempt to rise, Donna Rose Plumm trips over George and goes headlong into a clayey dark puddle. She shrills at George Jensen: "Idiot! Clumsy! Stupid! Pig!"

George looks sufficiently horrified, humbly apologizes, and meekly scurries away.

And Donna Rose Plumm's satiny white dress. All that deep-brown mud ground into it. It will be weeks and many washings before it can be worn again without a visible outline of mud stain.

Feckless George Jensen. He wanders back toward the schoolhouse, passing Mercy May along the way.

She winks at him, and he winks back. Maybe George Jensen isn't so clumsy after all. And he certainly has been redeemed for his dustup at second base with Mercy May two summers before.

And the very next day, the still-seething Donna Rose Plumm sits at her desk when James Richard passes by on a walk from the coat rack, ink bottle in hand. He too suffers from a spell of unexpected bumbling and butterfingeredness, and just how it happened, he could not exactly say under the stern cross-examination conducted by Mrs. Anne Durham; it just tragically came out that way, but the result was another raiment casualty for Donna Rose. Her dress was ruined, black splotches and spidery drips in a Rorschach backsplash against the pale-pink garment.

In sisterly sympathy, Mercy May tells the woebegone Donna Rose that if Mercy May only had another dress, and one large enough to fit Donna Rose, that she would gladly give it to her; but as Donna Rose already had observed and made public, Mercy May only had a single dress to her name and could, alas, be of no service. In sisterly commiseration, Mercy May further implies that it would be especially pleasing if a new dress were bright enough and bold enough to make the wart on her ear less noticeable to the general public. But not to worry. Didn't Donna Rose have one more school dress at home? Mercy May suggests.

A floral-patterned green dress with a frilly collar? And wasn't it her newest and nicest dress?

Donna Rose quakes in anger, but she is no fool. She is, of course, a church choir president in the making and already understands the great expectations to which she has been foreordained. She has made the calculation that she has but one dress left, and it may be in considerable jeopardy of falling victim to an unknown threat from a shiftless and cunning enemy. She decides to offer no resistance, acknowledge defeat, and accept the brief humiliation of being outwitted by a bunch of poor farm kids. If her last dress is ruined, she will be forced to wear the clothing of one of her brothers, a thought that sends quivers of horror up her spine. Her dislike of Mercy May, James Richard, and George Jensen still boils, but through her considerable willpower, she reduces the fire under the kettle to a mere simmer and there lets it remain. Perhaps there will be a time for avengement, but not now; the threesome is on high alert for a counterattack. Plus, she understands that revenge postponed only makes revenge sweeter.

So it is that Donna Rose Plumm becomes a diminished and humbled young woman, reduced to one wearable school dress for a time. She appears in it on Wednesday and then is forced to wear it again on Thursday. It is George Jensen who happens to comment, in an innocent voice just loud enough for the entire classroom to hear, at a quiet moment when the students are settling in for a rigorous day at school, "Isn't that the same dress you wore yesterday, Donna Rose?"

Anne Durham, her back to the class, writing the day's assignments on the chalkboard, hears George's observation. For a heartbeat, she considers investigating further into the matter and meting out justice, which surely is required. Then a small beguiling smile caresses her face, and she decides to just let it go. While she loves each of her students, it is fair to say that a few she esteems a little less than others. Among that small select group is Donna Rose Plumm, once-proud owner of three dresses, bossy as a farmyard hen, commander of classroom virtue.

Donna Rose had been overdue for a comeuppance.

***

At the Bell home late on Friday night, after the children and Arthur have retired, Mary heats a pot of water. She slips the Rit chips into it and watches the liquid turn a deep blue. Carefully, she slips Mercy May's one white dress in and stirs with a long skinny stick. Thirty minutes later, she pulls the dripping dress out and hangs it to dry in the wheezy desert air.

But her work is not yet done. Earlier in the day, she dug deep into her traveling trunk and pulled from it her wedding dress. Meticulously, she cut a three-inch-wide ribbon of white cloth from it and fashioned a graceful sash. When the dress dries and Mary attaches the sash, she is pleased with the results. More than pleased. Family honor and Mercy May's trouble have both been addressed and reconciled.

So it is that on Monday morning at school, even the captious Donna Rose Plumm takes note of Mercy May's appearance—her smile, her confidence, the white slender ribbon in her hair. Perhaps Donna Rose was mistaken; the Bell family is not as unsubstantial as she thought. After all, Mercy May is wearing a new navy-blue dress with a striking white sash.

Chapter Sixteen

EXPANSION OF THE BELL FAMILY home turns out to be a good project. When work for pay is scarce, a project at home nicely fills the void, and to boot, you have something to show for it. In the case of Arthur and Mary Bell, the result is a slightly larger house and a new room for Mercy May. Neither of them are people given to airs, but they occasionally take fleeting and small delight in imagined conversations among their neighbors: "You see that the Bells are adding a room to their place? Must be a room for their little girl. Maybe they're not doing so bad after all. Maybe they put aside a few dollars along the way."

Arthur and his sons have done well in acquiring the needed building materials. They've scouted, scrounged, and scraped for every piece of scrap wood between Filer and Buhl and hauled stone for the room's skirting. Arthur has wandered about two lumber companies and made himself known and occasionally useful; a couple of sturdy two-by-fours and a handful of nails for loading a wagon or truck is a satisfactory bargain for all concerns.

The roles of Arthur and Mary in the building of the room are quickly, if unconventionally, established. It is clear that Mary can envision, draw, and grasp the architectural demands, while Arthur and Lucas provide the steady, cheap labor. She lines out the plan in pencil on butcher paper in her small, precise hand. No detail escapes her, down to where the latch on the window will be and the placement of a doorstop. Arthur marvels at her natural mechanical ability, the way she sees space and then sees more, the way she pictures something in her mind in such a complete fashion and is able to transpose her vision in such a clear way.

If Noah needed an assistant to lay out the plan for the ark, Arthur muses, *my wife would have been more than able for the assignment.* And then he laughs a little to himself. Mary could plan it, he could build it, and Noah could husband the two-by-two of animals aboard.

So this addition takes on the flavor of their marital arrangement: a partnership, equal in every way but varied in responsibility and requirement. Mary becomes the supervisor and Arthur and his sons the crew. It proves a satisfactory arrangement.

They are heady days for Mercy May. Aunt Lollie Vanoy has sent another batch of magazines, and a bonus: a new pair of shoes that almost fit her and white anklets with thin red thread along the top. With her newly dyed dress, Mercy May feels as though she is among the most fortunate of all girls on the plain. And Aunt Lollie Vanoy has promised a new dress for Mercy May, soon to be shipped through the good office of the U.S. Postal Service. Two dresses! Mercy May feels as though she is a princess atop a throne fashioned of gold. She longs to meet her benefactress, Aunt Lollie Vanoy, and in her mind, she pictures how her distant relative must be: regal and royal, beneficent and kindly; a spiritual, lean, wise, and queenly presence watching over her from faraway Tennessee. In truth, Lollie Vanoy is a jowly, goodhearted, plump woman with fleshy arms, a bellowing laugh, and a booming personality; telltale signs of tobacco peek-a-booing on the corners of her mouth and wisps of gin on her breath in the evening. But Mercy May's imagination, while far from shore regarding her kin's physical appearance, is close to beach regarding her aunt's genuine concern for the branch of the family that has sprouted root and grown over the wall in faraway wild Idaho.

This clothing, with new wardrobe acquisitions courtesy Aunt Lollie Vanoy, is the clothing she dons for her much-anticipated trip with Mrs. Anne Durham to the library in Buhl: her deep-blue dress, the new shoes, and the anklets. Perched in the passenger seat of the somewhat ostentatious Buick, Mercy May has regal feelings of her own. *Nothing*, she thinks, *will ever compare to this Saturday morning trip to the library*—the public library, as it turns out, with wide welcoming doors bidding any and all to enter, poor, needy, and downtrodden included. She enters the library with reverence and trepidation, as an urchin would enter the temple of Zeus. Her breath comes in a gasp. She has never seen so many books. Rows and rows of them, the volumes stretching to the ceiling, most of them beyond her reach. Independent as can be, confident enough to fistfight George Jensen and mastermind a scheme to take down the haughty Donna Rose Plumm, Mercy May tenderly reaches for Anne Durham's hand. It is too much. It is more than she expected. She is overwhelmed. Anne Durham blushes and thinks of how lovely it would be someday to bear a daughter of her own.

"To the left, toward the corner, is where the young readers' section is. Maybe you'd like to start there, Mercy May. Pick out two or three books, and then we'll check them out and you can take them home. We'll come back a few Saturdays from now and return the books so you won't be assessed a late fee."

Mercy May listens with disbelief to Mrs. Durham. Revelation has not died with the last prophets of the New Testament. The chapter of libraries has been opened to her.

"I can take these books home to read?"

"Yes, of course. You check them out with a promise to return them," says Anne Durham, smiling. "The books are loaned to you. It is part of the services libraries provide."

Libraries must be the most wonderful places on the earth. The thought takes hold and swells within Mercy May. They are not the domain for only the wealthy. Someone—a great, wise, and good someone who understands human nature and the burning desire to read and read and then read some more—has determined that books can and should be taken home, a sacred trust. With aching humility and veneration nigh to a spiritual witness, Mercy May drops her hand from Anne Durham's and slowly walks to the young readers' section, not unlike Columbus first setting foot on the white sand and sighting the dusky tropical lushness of old Hispaniola, understanding that a new world beckons.

An hour later, Anne Durham encourages Mercy May to make her selections and walk to the front desk, where a library card will be issued and the books checked out. Unknown to Mercy May, Anne Durham has already paid the nickel fee for issuing a pale-green library card. Mercy May has made a fine selection of books: *Anne of Green Gables* and *Captains Courageous* and, after a foray into the adult section of the library, an irresistible choice, *Poems of Emily Dickinson*. For someone just turned nine, it is an impressive debut at the library. When she and Anne Durham next return to the building, Mercy May will have devoured all three books and committed to her wondrous memory a half dozen of Miss Dickinson's poems.

And what seems the best Saturday morning ever in her young life becomes even grander when Anne Durham leads Mercy May not to the sparkly Buick and back home but first to a small red-brick bakery and café, where the two eat soft round rolls splashed with sugary pink icing, and Mercy May swishes sweet orange juice around her mouth for the first time. Mercy May thinks the taste the most exquisite gastronomical experience ever.

For a half day, courtesy of Mrs. Anne Durham, Mercy May has escaped the hard times of a grinding existence. There is another world outside, a world of books and stories and promise, Mercy May realizes, although in phrasing suited to a nine-year-old. Farms can fail, people can go hungry, death can steal into a home at noon or midnight; families pack up what they can carry and disappear overnight, but there is more this world has to offer. There is something different and higher, there is hope, slender though the thread may be.

Mercy May's eyes are wide open. She knows the world a little better, and it is comforting, not frightening. She begins, on that Saturday morning, to see vast possibilities, both good and bad, but in her case, a slumbering native optimism comes alive, and it stays with her the remainder of her life, which is good; she will need to rely on that native optimism many more times during her peregrine journey on what proves to be a very long road. The seeds of hope and new worlds have been planted. It is what wise Anne Durham wanted to achieve with one simple trip to a small-town library.

***

When Anne Durham drives through the pale-green fields toward the teachers' home, she sees the Andrews brothers' wagon out front and their two husky forms unloading soil, shovel by shovel. Or she believes it to be soil, until she draws a bit closer and the wind changes direction in the slight, and she recognizes it not to be soil at all.

"Good day to you, Mrs. Anne," Tom calls out in a note as cheerful as a meadowlark's June song.

"A mighty purty day it is too," chimes in Ben, thrusting his shovel into the fetid, smutty mound.

It is the Andrews brothers' apex, their culmination, their capstone, their climax, their finest offering in order to secure the Buick for their picnic date, which, they ingenuously assume, will propel them toward a life of blissful matrimony.

It is the gift of cow manure.

"They just showed up this morning, Anne. I had not the slightest idea they would be at our doorstep soon after you departed," Daniel explains when she steps inside the teacherage, a mite of apology in his voice, huddling inside the house as the Andrews brothers hustle around outside, the doors and windows of the house shut in a feeble attempt to keep the smell of fusty, foul excrement from invading.

"They talked about gardens—how it was time to put one in, how gardens have saved many people from hunger and deprivation around here. Then it was Ben, I think, although I can hardly tell them apart, who said, 'You plan to put in a garden, Mr. Durham?' Trying to be neighborly and not wanting to appear the eastern slacker, I assented and said yes, we were toying with the idea.

"Then the other one smiled, a ridiculous grin if I've ever seen one, and said, 'We'll fix you up. We'll get you started good and proper.' Next thing I know, they've plowed up a half acre, run some contraption over it to smooth the soil, and they're now mixing in what I take to be horse or cattle dung. Honestly, Anne, what was I to do? It happened so suddenly. I was taken in before I could utter a protest."

Anne can see the bewilderment in her husband's eyes. Clearly, he had been overwhelmed and overmatched by the exuberant brothers and their desire to share the richness of manure.

"I'll go see what I can find out." She sighs. "That odor. Oh my goodness. I don't think I can ever get used to it."

She steps onto the porch and is greeted cheerily by the brothers, both dressed in plaid shirts peeking from behind bib overalls, straw hats on their heads, and sunny dispositions all around.

"Afternoon, Mrs. Durham," they chime, as if rehearsed.

"I want to thank you two for the . . . the work that you've performed today. Daniel says you're starting a garden for us."

"We are starting a garden—" Tom says.

"For the two of you—" Ben joins in.

"So that you'll have extra food to eat—" adds Tom.

"And be able to neighbor better," Ben completes.

"Neighbor better?" Anne asks, not sure what to do with a noun clothed as a verb.

"Yep, neighbor," Ben starts. "You go out and neighbor in the fall. You show up with corn in hand or tomatoes or peas or—"

"What have you," says Tom. "That's one of the ways folks know you're good people. You neighbor with them when the garden comes in. We hope you don't mind."

Anne understands what her husband faced. A tidal wave of help and cordiality, a whirlwind of good intentions, an erupting volcano of . . . of . . . neighboring. She could no more stop the Andrews twins from establishing a garden plot than she could hold up her hand and reverse the course of the Snake River. To neighbor. Anne Durham understands the meaning.

She falls back to the most immediate and potentially aggravating concern, the malodorous fumes rising from the overturned soil.

"And how long will the . . . the . . . well, you know, the smell of manure be with us?" she asks in as polite and diplomatic tone as possible. She does not, under any circumstance, want to topple the newly constructed bridge of neighboring with the Andrews.

"Oh, it goes away in time," Ben says. "After a while, you hardly notice it."

"I think it smells kind of good," Tom pitches in. "You know. It reminds you that things are growing and that you're on the land and how one thing can help another and that nothin' should go to waste."

"Even waste," Ben says, and both brothers cackle. "You oughtn't waste waste."

By now, Anne, too, has hoisted the flag of surrender, overwhelmed by the effusive benevolence of the two young men. She and Daniel will have a garden. In fact, it's already well underway. They *will* grow crops. Upon harvest, they *will* share crops with others. And in that small way, they *will* become a little more part of the community fabric, take part in the rural economy of the plain, and further prove their credentials as Idahoans, not Pennsylvanians. In short, they *will* neighbor. *All in all,* Anne thinks, *it's probably a good bargain.* And the Andrews. Who could resist them and their wonderful intentions?

She offers the weak and common response to the brothers' overpowering kindness.

"If there is anything Daniel or I can do to repay your thoughtfulness . . ."

And with those vapid, throwaway few words, she walks straight into the trap the brothers have placed square in the path she treads. The floodgate opens, and the water thrashes through.

The brothers look at each other and mightily try, and for the most part fail, to suppress a pair of goofy, cat-got-the-mouse grins.

"Well, Mrs. Durham, since you mentioned it—"

"There is one little thing that we—"

"Would like to ask you about—"

"If it's okay with you—"

"Only on the condition that it's really okay with you—"

"And also that Mr. Daniel likes the idea too—"

"Yeah, of course, he needs to be part of it—"

"That is to say—"

"We'd like it very much—"

"If we could borrow the Buick because—"

"We got dates," Tom says earnestly. "Dates with girls," he adds triumphantly.

"We figger it's time for us to do some courtin'," Ben says limply, and the tone of his voice touches Anne Durham, in no small part because it wasn't long ago that she and Daniel were courting too, and she has been in southern Idaho long enough to know that a farm or ranch can only carry a man so far.

"We're of a certain age," Tom picks up the chatter. "An age where we think we need to maybe each take us a wife. Not that we don't get along good—"

"Because we do," Ben interjects. "As good as any brothers, and I think I would have liked Tom even if we weren't brothers—"

"But it's just a good thing, and natural too, that we cut out the flirtin' and court more than we have," Tom says.

"Which, if you're talkin' practical, is no courtin' at all," Ben says. "We've spent an overly amount of time working the farm."

"So we had this idea to ask out a couple of girls—"

"Naomi Kendricks and Chloe Perkins, both real nice girls, even though Chloe's father, Squat, is mostly a stupid cuss—"

"And we thought, well, this is what we thought. If we were to drive up in a car, say a nice Buick, and take them out on a date, why, they'd most likely be impressed."

"Mighty impressed."

"And if they're impressed, it would bode good for us, and maybe we'd get around to marrying them sometime and having babies and whatnot."

"So that's our case, Mrs. Durham. All right there, and we would've done all these nice things for you anyway—"

"But we figgered it would make it easier for you to say yes if you were a little in debt to us," perorates Ben in a blankly honest, beguiling way. Then both brothers in unison chant, "Please?"

Anne Durham has listened to the conversation with amazement and an inner squeaky bemusement. She looks at the brothers, in their plaid shirts, bib overalls, straw hats in hand, arms held wide, apprehension and hope on their faces. She thinks one or both of them might just pass out if she doesn't provide an answer right away, a scenario she does not wish to deal with.

"Well, Tom and Ben," she says contemplatively. "I'd like to neighbor with you as well, even if you hadn't been so helpful to Daniel and me of late. Our car is your car. When would you like to borrow the Buick?"

***

So the plans of the Andrews brothers, the Andrews bachelors, take a leap forward. All they have to do next is arrange a date with Miss Kendricks and Miss Perkins, a milestone not as fretsome as they feared it might be. All that is left is the asking.

Mr. and Mrs. Edwin Kendricks seem overjoyed that a handsome and successful young farmer such as Tom Andrews is interested in their Naomi. The Kendrickses are good people, maybe great people, assiduous and tender in their attention and guidance to their children and to each other, but they are also tired. At nineteen, Naomi is the eldest of eleven children, and they secretly equate Tom

Andrews's affections for her as possibly one less mouth to feed, one less child to clothe, one less daughter's fortunes to worry about. Oh, they certainly will miss her help with the younger children, for Naomi is as maternal and kindhearted as any young woman can be, but from their vast reservoir of children, the next daughter in line, Zina, can step into the breach and perform as admirably.

And besides, the Kendrickses are worn down. Eleven children always mean a long, toilsome day for father and mother. It was Jo Powell who once remarked to a clerk in the grocery, "None of my business, but I just wish Edwin would leave his wife alone more than he does," but that is not the way it turned out. Camille Kendricks, at age forty, would deliver a final child in a year hence, and the couple's goal of parenting an even dozen offspring is realized.

"Yep, Tom, go right ahead and court Naomi as you please," was Edwin Kendricks's quick and unequivocal response when the handsomer of the Andrews twins sought permission to call upon her.

For Ben, it was a slightly bumpier road. Fractious Squat Perkins acted true to nature. Not even the long-term welfare of his daughter could budge him.

"Chloe. Well now," Squat Perkins almost spits out the words, annoyance and irritability creased into his stubbly, leathery face. "She's barely seventeen and a source of unending joy to me and her mother. Still just a child in most ways. Why, just this mornin' she says to me, 'Papa, could I fix you some eggs for breakfast? And bacon too?' She's a devoted one, that little girl. I'd miss her terrible if she was ever to leave home. Yes, still a tender, sweet child." And he feigns wiping a nonexistent tear from his left eye.

Chloe is actually two months shy of twenty, a fact that Ben knows well, but his uncommon good sense forbids him to correct Squat Perkins.

"I don't know. I just don't know," Squat Perkins laments. "Not all grown-up, even. Just a child, a sweet child." And his face was long and sad, and he pulled a grimy handkerchief from his pocket and blew his nose. "So innocent. Just a baby."

"It's just for a date, Squat. I ain't askin' for her hand in marriage," Ben protests mildly, although in his head he tags on to the end of his sentence, "at least for now."

Squat Perkins looks every bit the part of a man well-acquainted with sorrow and grief, an Atlas of the plain, the world perched on his shoulders. He gazes toward the sky as though seeking some divine signal, although his communion with heaven is generally limited to blue invectives when his hammer slams his thumb or a cow kicks over the milk bucket.

And then it comes. The lever sought by Squat, hoped for by Ben.

"You still got that mare, five years old or so, I reckon?" he asks in a voice that sounds almost pained.

"Sure do, if you mean the one we call Queenie."

"Yes, I believe that's the one. Say, Ben, why don't you bring that horse around sometime and let me take a look at her? Maybe you can do that before you call on Chloe. Fair enough?"

"Yes, sir, fair enough. I'll do that. It'd be my pleasure."

And Ben walks away from Squat Perkins knowing that if he is to move forward with Chloe, it's going to cost him one of his best horses.

But Ben is astute enough to recognize it's more than a fair trade.

So the day for the date is set: Saturday, May 13, 1934. The arrangements are made.

Now all the Andrews brothers need to do is allow their handsomeness, success, and native charm win over the hearts of Naomi Kendricks and Chloe Perkins.

To them, it seems the easiest step of all. They've seen it played out a million times on their farm with livestock, in the mountains and rangeland with game, and among their once-bachelor friends on the plain. Love, it seems, is easy enough. It is only natural.

***

Spring's feeling of joyful expectedness extends to others on the plain, including Reverend Ennis Popplestone. He walks, rickety-spindle, along a country road on a Saturday afternoon, dressed in dark pants, a white shirt, and a black tie, attire he feels is appropriate for a country parson as he calls upon his sheep. His ministry is still defined by the urge to walk about and do good, and his Saturday afternoon ramblings have become a highlight of his week. Most people welcome him gladly. A few don't. Some lay their burdens at his feet. A few take them away. Some repent and vow to do better at his gentle urging. Most don't. Some promise to return to church. A few actually do. All in all, it is a rewarding time for him.

In the right pocket of his black pants, he carries a letter from home—Iowa— signed by his father. He pulls the letter out and begins to read it for the second time, and the combination of walking and reading on a cloddy road gives his gait even more of a herky-jerky visage.

Dearest Son,

We hope our letter to you is a welcome sight! We so worry about you in faraway Idaho and wish we were closer. Your mother misses you so, as do your Brother and

Sisters. Mother's pillow is wet from her tears some nights, and all I can do is hold her and comfort her by saying you are doing God's work and He must have a plan for you.

We hope you are well and indeed doing the work of the Lord. We hope you have Friends and are making many goodly acquaintances, especially with some fine Young Ladies of a marriageable disposition. You are a fine-looking lad, and I am sure you have your pick of them. If you are thinking in a Matrimonial way, we hope that we get the chance to meet the Young Lady before or soon after you wed. Can you perform your own Marriage ceremony? Ha! Now that would be one told around the supper table for years to come.

We are all well at home and wish you to not worry about us. Your letters are richly welcomed here and cause for all of us to gather 'round and read each word ever so carefully. Your Brother, I think, misses you almost as much as your Mother. He so looks up to you. But you have set a fine example for him, and I have high Fatherly hopes that he will be as good a boy—no, now I must say "man"—as you are. Your Mother and I cannot ask for anything more.

I must now take care of chores and then go to work, for which I am thankful. Through all of these Times, it has been a blessing to have an income, meager though it may be. Mr. Phelps could have given me the slip, but he had kept me on because he is a Good and Kind man. We get by and thank God for our blessings, the food on our table, the clothes on our backs, the good health of our Family and Friends.

I leave you now with all the tenderness and loving thoughts that a Father is capable of and trust you are strong and feel well and helping others along. You know you would be welcome at home any time, although we also understand you are doing His work in the great vineyard of Idaho. God be with you, my sweet and wonderful Son.

Your loving Father,
Leon

Young Reverend Popplestone halts his uneven walk and stares at the letter and then carefully folds it and puts it back in his pocket and thinks of how he detests being so far from his home and family. He looks north toward the Centennial Mountains, still with a crest of snow on the highest peaks. He turns his head and gazes into the late afternoon sunshine, a hand cupped over his eyes. He sees the next house along the road to the west and kicks up only a little dust as he begins the long walk toward it.

At the same instant, in a small town in Iowa, a humble father closes his eyes and imagines his son, a son who does not walk backroads with a flappy, awkward gait, but as a strong young man who moves with grace, purpose, and conviction, fearless and agile. A John the Baptist, a Peter, a Paul, or so he thinks. And because the father loves his son so much, what he sees behind closed eyes is real.

***

An hour later, he hears the purring of an engine and sees who he believes are Tom and Ben Andrews rumbling down the road in the Durham's big new Buick. The car sways and jolts as it makes its way toward Ennis Popplestone, who is unsure if the automobile is being driven by the Andrews or if it's the other way around.

"Reverend, can we give you a lift somewhere?" one of them shouts, though the preacher is never quite sure which brother is which.

"No thanks, boys. The walk is doing me good. It allows me to think some." Then, taking note of the Buick, he says, "Where you two headed in that fancy car?"

"We're going to pick up—"

"Two girls, and we're heading out on a picnic."

"We've got ourselves—"

"Dates. With girls. Pretty girls."

"Which is what you'd expect of us, since we're both so handsome."

"Although, I am handsomer than him."

"No, you aren't."

Spindly Reverend Popplestone enjoys the banter, wishes the boys good luck, and slyly adds, "Of course, you know I perform weddings," to which both Andrews brothers hoot and cackle and promise him their business should everything work out. And then they pull away, still chortling, two merry men with matrimonial ambitions, on a mission.

And then, since he has miles to go and plenty of time to think, Ennis Popplestone feels a pang in his chest and wonders, as does his father, if he ever will, on this river plain, meet fine young ladies of a marriageable disposition.

***

It has gone so well, so very well, for the Andrews twins. Their original plan changed a tad; rather than drive all the way to the north side of Twin Falls to Blue Lakes for their picnic, they'd decided on a pleasant, flat patch of ground south of Filer, where a creek that sprouted high in the Jarbidges burbled its way toward the Snake. Blue Lakes, Ben and Tom decided, was a decent spot for a Saturday picnic, but it's where people commonly go for such an outing, and on this, their first dates with girls they have long admired, they sought more originality, a place more memorable than where many others went. In years to come, if all worked out, they wanted the young ladies they were with, by then their wives, to look at the glade off the country road, across the meadow, near the creek, under the shade of linty cottonwood trees and remember it as *their* place, the spot where romance budded and blossomed. It is admirable foresight for two young men who rarely think beyond the day's tasks and chores and the downward price spiral of crops and livestock.

So the blanket was spread, the food arrayed and picked at through the languid afternoon. Happy chatter, merry laughter, punctuated by obvious flirting from man to woman and reciprocated from woman to man. The brothers are both dreamy and euphoric; their charm so thick that they imagine it even overshining the happy brook. They wish for the afternoon, and then the early evening, to slow, to linger and last, for the minutes to seem as pleasant hours. The Andrews brothers are blissfully unaware of anything other than the narrow scope of the world set forth on the plaid blanket and the remnants of a fried chicken, potato salad and cherry pie picnic luncheon and the enchanting company of Naomi Kendricks and Chloe Perkins.

Dizzied by the moment, Ben thinks he would gladly give up ten mares of Queenie's stature for the chance to hold Chloe's hand and kiss her goodnight. The brothers dream away the afternoon, leaving their world behind and taking the two young ladies with them.

Which may account for them not noticing the skies taking on a blue-and-purple tint to the south over the mountains, where spring thunderstorms form, bound for the Snake River Plain. The notoriously changeable plain weather is about to deal them an unexpected hand.

There is devilry in the sky. A staticky fork of lightning, the boom of thunder, the sweep of the rain line seeming to take dead aim on the picnickers. Flighty Idaho weather has broken the spell of the brothers' otherwise superb, dreamy day.

"I suppose we'd better gather things up and get to the car," Ben says morosely as the first fat raindrops splat onto the ground.

So the four gather the remnants of their picnic, and while it takes only minutes to do so, it is sufficient time for the thick drops to turn into a sheet of rain.

And the sheet of rain quickly turns the paradisiacal meadow into a muddy gumbo.

And no Buick, from that time until today, is a match for the slippery, treacherous southern Idaho gumbo.

The wheels zizz and groan and spin, and Tom looks at Ben and Ben looks at Tom and Chloe looks at Naomi and Naomi looks at Chloe. There are few feelings as lonely and helpless as being away from home, night about to fall, huddled in an automobile, and no seeable way out. They have been cast from the garden and ordered to look eastward.

So they wait. The thunderstorm proves to be like most in that part of the country: it rages and seethes and lashes the land below for forty-five minutes.

And then, as suddenly as it started, it stops. As if in apology, a rainbow arcs to the east, brilliant against the almost-dark sky.

Tom looks outside the car window, feeling pressure to come up with a solution, a magical act that will transport them from this place to that in a blink of the eye. But he cannot, nor can his brother, and the regal, aristocratic Buick remains as idle as Coleridge's painted ship upon a painted ocean.

"Any ideas, Ben?"

"Yeah. Just one. And one of us ain't gonna like it."

"Get out and push?"

"I don't see how we can get around it."

Chloe Perkins says, "We can wait here. Someone's bound to come by, and we can ask for help."

Naomi Kendricks says, "We can get out and push too."

The Andrews twins dismiss both suggestions. The first requires patience and tenacity, qualities in short supply between the brothers. At this point in life, they cumulatively have the emotional range of a rooting hog. And it takes the rescue away from them and places it in the hands of strangers or, perhaps worse, friends who would remind them for years of the predicament, never in a kindly manner. And the thought of the two young women, though both of them well-acquainted with hard work and solving problems, getting behind the automobile and pushing offends the brothers' sensibilities, not to mention pinches their male pride. They got themselves into this mess and, by golly, they will find a way out of it.

Ben takes a fifty-cent piece out of his pocket and looks at Tom.

"Heads or tails?"

He flips the coin in the air as his brother calls out, "Tails."

"Tails it is. You steer, I push."

Ben reluctantly takes off his jacket, his shirt, his shoes, and his socks and slides out the door and into the clayey goo. Tom, who was already in the driver's seat, starts the Buick's engine, and the results are both predictable and futile: Ben returns encased in the gumbo and looking mummified in mud, and the car has, for all its whining and spinning wheels, moved not an inch. In fact, it has settled a little deeper into what seems its muddy grave. And since he is so filthy, he dares not slide back into the Buick and nuzzle up against his beloved Chloe.

They are stuck. Stuck in the mud. Stuck for ideas. Stuck for a plan.

Naomi offers, "I can slide over and steer. I can drive a tractor, so I don't think there'd be much difference with a car. That way, both of you can push, and maybe that will get us out of here."

Clean Tom doesn't much like the idea, especially in light of how his brother looks, but he can't think of a reason or excuse that would be accepted as honorable in the girls' eyes. Much as Jonas returning to Ninevah, with a silent pout and cerebral protest, he removes shirt, socks, shoes, and rolls up his pants and joins his brother in the muddy fray, with the same results: a rooster tail of slosh and slop flying from the back tires and sticking to Tom like wet cement. Now both Andrewses are banned from the Buick.

The light to the west has faded and slipped away. The rainbow long gone. It soon will be moonless black. Already, the girls are late reporting home. Ben wonders what kind of greeting he'll receive from Squat Perkins, traipsing up to the doorway at midnight, caked in mud. He wonders, but he knows. He thinks the asking price for Chloe may have leaped to two horses. Maybe more. And the Durhams are doubtlessly worried about the Buick and second-guessing themselves about loaning it to the hayseed brothers.

This is the picture: Two young ladies in picnic dresses, ribbons in their hair, sit idly in the car, while two brothers sit in the mud, backs against the Buick, and mourn. Mourn over a good day gone wrong, mourn over reputations gone sour, mourn over being made to feel stupid by a thunderstorm, the slick Idaho soil, and a sleek Buick that seemed content to go nowhere. Mourn over marriages that might have been and children held back in heaven.

Ben finally says, "I'd best get walking. I think Dave Hamilton's place isn't too far away. Maybe I could talk him into a team of horses and figure out some kind of rigging to get us pulled out of here. Ol' Dave's always been good to us. I think he'd go along with it."

Tom sighs and says, "You should get on your way. I'll stay here with the girls."

So it is that just before midnight, those stranded in a muddy meadow hear the jangling of reins and the practiced tone of Ben's voice driving a pair of big-backed horses toward the car. Naomi long ago had crawled over to the back seat of the Buick and joined in sisterly companionship with Chloe. They both doze peacefully until awakened by the tromping horses, as Ben mumbles curses, berating himself for not seeing the cobalt cloud headed toward the meadow. Though a rarity for the feisty brothers, they indulge in a rare case of self-pity.

Not much more remains to be said of the date-turned-disaster. After considerable fussing and heavy labor, the horses extract the Buick from the mud, and the animals return to their wry owner. The Buick itself will be left outside the teachers' home as the sky shows a hint of orange and yellow to the east and the morning songbirds begin to trill. On the front seat will be a scribbled note promising a thorough cleaning of the car and a stout explanation of how it became so dirty. By the time the Andrews twins return to clean the car, the tale will have already taken a humorous turn, and while Ben and Tom wash and scrub the Buick, Anne and Daniel Durham will be treated to a rollicking account of the night's events. Among the Andrews's endearing characteristics is the ability to find humor in any situation, especially if they are the objects of the joke. So that is that. That is it. A joke on themselves.

Except. One more calamity occurs that fateful night. When Ben holds the car door open for Chloe to exit, he slips, and they both fall on account of poor footing from the same slickening rainstorm that had mired the Buick. The number of people caked in mud instantly increases by one.

Trying to salvage a shred of gallantry, Ben says, "I'll just carry you to the house so that you won't get any more dirty. If I slip and go down, at least you'll have something soft to land on." And with no protest from Chloe, he hoists her into his burly arms and tracks to the front porch. It is just after five in the morning.

And on the porch, grizzled and grumpy and not having good thoughts about mankind in general and Ben Andrews in particular, Squat Perkins sits with a shotgun nestled on his lap. He surveys the scene: Mud-caked man, about half-dressed, carrying his mud-caked daughter, her hair askew, her skirt scandalously hiked up to almost her knees, her arms around his neck.

And red-eyed Squat Perkins snorts, pulls the shotgun to his chest, glowers in the darkness of the wee morning hours, his odor of sweat, soil, and anger, and snarls, "I'm sure you have a story, boy. And it had darned well better be a good one."

***

Their dream was this. Their dream went just like this: Two brothers and their wives. At Sunday supper on a late summer day. Children all around. Cousins. Playing with each other under the shade of big trees on a grassy lawn. Happy chatter in the air. Lots of food and good feelings. A decent harvest in the offing. Two men, a little silver in their hair, now stout, one of them walking with a limp, taking it all in, their wives close by, telling merry stories to everyone who will listen, which is all but the very youngest. Their names are Ben and Tom, and nearby are Chloe and Naomi.

And it is a dream that came true, down to the smallest detail, including telling the favorite family story of them all, about the time when the four young adults, way back when, got stuck in a borrowed Buick during a gulley-washer of a storm, and how one of them had to do some quick and fancy talking to avoid getting his head blown off by Grandpa Perkins.

Chapter Seventeen

SHE HAS FIVE GRANDDAUGHTERS, AND even with the plagues of old age, she has not missed one of their weddings, though it has meant, in instances, considerable travel, uncomfortably completed.

It is the youngest of her granddaughters who weds this day, in Idaho, one hundred miles east of where she grew up. The western end of the Jarbidge Mountains rise above the plain, little nubs barely above the horizon. The same Snake River of her girlhood flows a dozen miles to the south of where the wedding occurs. Mountains, plains, rivers, memories, and headstones mark this place as her true home.

The wedding finished, the reception begins. Guests form a line, long and snaky, and offer wishes of warmth, happiness, and posterity to the young couple. Not far from where the newlyweds stand, she sits on an overstuffed chair, walker beside her, near the fireplace on this chill November night. You cannot miss her: See her there, to the side, the perpetual smile of delight at being present at the event; her perfectly coiffed white hair; the pink dress—yes, it must be pink, it has to be pink; she is, after all, Mercy May—and the radiance emanating from her, as unmistakable as the bride in her white dress, the jazzy music, the pleasant buzz of conversation. She is the star of the evening. After the party winds down, even the bride acknowledges that her grandmother stole the show. Well-wishers stroll through the formal reception line and then, almost to a person, they stop and talk to this glorious elderly lady, this bolt of white sunshine, whether they have met her previously or not.

And though the words are difficult to form—we wonder if she has not suffered other, undetected strokes—she smiles munificently and speaks with slurred words to everyone. She is regal in her grace, admired in her beauty, venerated for her white-haired wisdom.

And people are so kind to her.

"Back to Idaho. You made it back to Idaho for a wedding," I say to her. "Home at last."

"Yes . . . home. At last," she says. She often repeats the last part of what has just been spoken to her, perhaps because the words are fresh in her mind.

The reception is almost over, and as I have done periodically through the day, I come to check on her, to see how she is doing. As far as I can determine, she is doing well, holding up better than, say, the bride's father.

She speaks again, this time with no prompting by another's words.

"I have not . . . been here in . . . Idaho . . . too often," she says. "When I left . . . I left. And Mother didn't live long . . . just another ten years or so. Her heart. The fever. What . . . do you call it? Oh my. Words . . . words . . . words. Rheumatic fever. Yes . . . that's it . . . it made her heart weak. How weak, we . . . didn't . . . understand 'til . . . later."

It's almost eleven o'clock.

"We'd better get you back to the hotel," I suggest. "It's been a long day."

"Yes . . . I am a . . . little tired."

"Your handsome grandson Christopher can take you."

"Oh . . . that would be fine. He . . . is quite . . . handsome. If he were only a sailor . . . and not my grandson . . . I would be sure . . . to flirt with him. And his younger brother, too."

The arrangements are made to transport her. A mischievous look crosses her features. She is the Mercy May of old, the one who wanted to fight George Jensen, the youngster who took down the snooty Donna Rose Plumm, the World War II bride who would see her young husband off to war twice, the widow at fifty-two when her sailor husband died of bone cancer, the woman who endured more than a dozen surgeries herself and fought back from a stroke that would have killed almost every other human her age; it all comes back to her, and she asks my son, "Would you mind . . . Christopher . . . if we stopped and picked up a . . . cheeseburger? I'm a little hungry."

We all laugh, but sure enough, she gets her midnight cheeseburger.

Tomorrow, I will take her to the airport, along with one of my sisters, who serves as her caretaker, company, and chaperone on this trip. She will look at me just before the car stops at the departing passenger terminal and dreamily, softly say, "You know, I have missed them so much. It will be so good . . . to see them again."

I do not need to ask of whom she speaks. She speaks of Mother and Father, the brothers who went before her. She speaks of her husband. She speaks of Scrappy and Juanita Burroughs, of the Andrews twins, of Jo Powell, of Frederic Bowker, of Ennis Popplestone, of Anne and Daniel Durham, of George Jensen, of Ken Bailey. She speaks of them all and more.

Shadows and ghosts, ghosts and shadows. But pleasant memories they all are.

I help her out of the car and to the door leading to the airline's check-in area. I can still hear the click, click, clicking of her walker, tapping her way away. I can still see her pause, look over her shoulder, and slowly raise her hand to wave goodbye.

It is the last time I see my mother alive.

Chapter Eighteen

IT COMES TO, IT COMES to, it all comes to this for a young girl growing up on the southern Idaho Plain: a vile mawing cloud rumbling in from the west that splatters sorrow on the home of Arthur and Mary Bell. The marking event of her young life, which will set her character forever.

***

Work on the new room moves ahead, and Mercy May's excitement grows by the day. All the materials are on hand and the design is complete. Arthur, for the twentieth time, answers the persistent question from Mercy May: "When will it be done?"

This time, he has a firm date in mind, now that the foundation is down, the river rock is set, and the room is framed. "Three weeks, Mercy May. Three more weeks, and we'll move you away from those hooligan brothers of yours and get you into a room fit for a young lady."

And there is more good news. A farmer on the other side of Buhl, named Grayson, is hiring a bit, and Arthur has sporadic work. The first handful of dollar bills hasn't shown up yet, but Phillip Grayson has a good name, and no one is worried about him keeping his word. Privately, Mary determines to stuff twenty-two dollars and eighty-seven cents back into the sugar-bowl-turned-bank-vault, matching its high-water mark before Arthur and Bowker bought Scrappy Burroughs's Farmall tractor.

Lucas hears of a CCC camp getting organized for the next year near Hagerman. He's almost of age to sign up. Building roads and constructing livestock watering ponds will be the unit's main task, and rumor says the camp superintendent, a man named Hoff, is a sports fanatic and will put together a baseball team. In his mind, Lucas sees himself patrolling center field or flinging the horsehide from shortstop to the first sacker. There are even whispers of a swimming pool, which prove true, although it turns out to be little more than a glorified mud hole on the east side of camp.

But the pay. Lucas goes over it in his mind again and again. Thirty dollars a month, twenty-five of which is required to be sent home, which certainly will help. Food, a bed, work clothes, and five dollars at his disposal. A dollar a day and a place to lay his head, and help for family at home. It is a good life, almost too much for Lucas to hope for. And in return, all he needs to do is work hard, something he already knows how to do.

And Sam and Silas are big enough now to hire out for a day here and there when school lets out. Maybe they'd only bring home a quarter or half dollar, but it all will go into the sugar bowl. The garden responsibilities will belong to James Richard and Mercy May.

The Bell family has a plan.

It's fair to say that a spirit of optimism sprouts and grows that spring of 1934 among the Bells. The clouds have given way to thin shafts of sunshine spearing down from the heavens to touch the earth. F. D. R. has the country on track again. More people are going to work, bringing checks home, buying a little more. The soil is good, rich, and warm and needs only water to produce lush and verdant fields. Prices are still ridiculously low and the middleman still rakes in far too much, but those conditions can't last forever, can't even last long. There's a sense of money to be made, enough to pull them out of the wretched hole of their poverty.

On a Friday night in late April, Arthur jangles three quarters in his pocket, a bit of pay from Grayson, announces he's hungry for sweets, and to Mercy May's and Mary's astonishment, scoops up his family, loads them on the wagon, and drives in high spirits and mirth all the way to Buhl for ice cream. Mercy May remembers the strawberry ice cream that night as the best she's ever had.

The sun is up, the doubts pushed back. A feeling that seems a little like hope crawls on its belly into the Bell's small house, curls up in a corner, and takes residence.

And then it all goes away, and life for the Bells again turns hard and dirty, because Arthur dies.

***

Tick fever. Common enough, treatable. Arthur often came home with ticks on his arms, legs, and back after a springtime day working the fields. Forty-three was his record, and Mary was well acquainted with lighting a match, heating a knife blade, and sticking the point of it under the rump end of the tick and watching the ugly brute of a bug raise itself high enough to be plucked off and plopped into a jar of alcohol.

Arthur, like his wife, seldom complains, but over a few days' period, lets it be known that he is feeling tired and feverish. But Grayson depends on him, the money is needed, so he pulls himself up each morning and goes to work. It is part of the family plan.

Then comes a turn. He grows listless and words come slowly, and his bloated face takes on a dullness that makes him seem almost a stranger to his family. This is not Arthur. This is wrong. Work on the house addition, the room for his beloved Mercy May, halts.

The gnawing pit in Mercy May's stomach begins to expand, enveloping her chest, her heart, her spine, her mind. A steady sense of sharp dread wells up the way a snow drift mounts in January outside the back door.

"Not tonight, Mercy May," he tells her in a sluggish tone, his eyes closed, the bit of red rash running up his neck and along his arms. "No. No thanks. You and Mr. Browning and Miss Dickinson are on your own," and then he excuses himself and shuffles painfully to his bed.

The rash grows and turns savage in the next three days. Arthur comes home at noon, barely able to move, hardly able to speak. The lines on Mary's face begin to deepen, and her face turns to chalk.

"We can take you to the hospital, Arthur, please," Mary begs. "You're looking worse. You can barely move. You're of no use to Mr. Grayson."

"Just got to run its course," Arthur says heavily, slumped in a chair, breathing hard.

"You have tick fever. There's medicine. You can be treated."

"It's all right, Mary."

This is part of it: Arthur is stubborn and he is proud and he has no money and he'd rather suffer through illness than go into any man's debt. The sugar bowl is empty, aside from pennies and a few nickels. He has only himself to blame, resulting from his unlikely partnership with Bowker to purchase the Farmall for his friend Scrappy Burroughs. And the other part of it: He is so tired. So weary. So fatigued. A trip all the way to Buhl seems the same as asking him to climb a Himalayan peak.

Later that night, Mercy May hears the muffled conversation.

The thick tone of her father: "We haven't any, dear. You know that."

The gritty voice of her mother: "We'll find some. The boys are working. Be reasonable."

"I just need some rest. No tick will kill me," came Arthur's feeble voice.

"Please. For us. Put aside your foolish pride."

"I can't. Couldn't scrape together five dollars if my life depended on it."

"Maybe it does, Arthur."

"Let me rest. I need to go to work tomorrow. Grayson won't pay me if I don't," Arthur mumbles. "He's no Scrappy Burroughs. No work, no pay. The old skinflint."

And the conversation dims. Until two in the morning.

Mary grasps Mercy May's arm and shakes it, not gently, but with purpose and strength.

"Daddy's taken a turn for the worse. I'm going to have Lucas and Sam get him to the wagon and take him to the hospital."

Mercy May jolts awake and scrambles to the front door, where she hears sounds that frighten her. Voices from Lucas and Sam, encouraging their father; the heavy, thudding step of Arthur; Mary's worried voice—"A few steps more, dear. A few steps more"; the horse Jenks pawing at the ground, as if wondering why he has been called to duty at this odd hour.

And she glimpses a sight that will imprint in her mind forever, a sight so horrible, so poignant, so unexpected that it propels her into a shocked state: her father, febrile, red-faced, rashy, propped under each arm by his oldest sons, barely dragging himself toward the waiting wagon. With horror, yet unerring perception, Mercy May understands her father is dying from within.

He lurches forward and tries to steady himself on the wagon's flank, but his hands miss; only with gentle pushing from his sons is he laid in the back of the wagon on a thick blanket. Arthur moans, a deep sigh of agony that pierces the early hour as it carries across the plain. Mercy May can bear no more. She sprints through the house and to the side of the wagon, hoists herself up, and peers in. In confusion, Arthur looks up to see his only daughter's face, and he rallies for a moment. He tries to speak, but thick tongue, delirium, and pain prevent him from doing so. Mercy May feels helpless. She does not know what to do, what to say, whom she should comfort—her father, her mother, her brothers, herself—and wishes for words, words, any kind of words that would be meaningful, would be remembered, words that would ease the strain on the gathering of lost souls at the wagon. Her precious words. They must come. And then she remembers. She remembers the Dickinson book from the library, and in the cool spring night, at the moment of test and experience and what later will prove to be the birth of a new and dark understanding, she recites:

> *The world is just a little place,*
> *just the red in the sky before the sun rises;*

so let us keep fast hold of hands,
that when the birds begin,
none of us be missing.

Arthur looks her way and whispers his thanks. And then Lucas climbs on to the wagon and gently prods Jenks and steers the wagon toward town and the hospital.

***

Mary watches. She watches the wagon and the dim shape of her two eldest sons silhouetted in the feeble light from the small house. She watches them carry away her husband, and she knows she will not likely see him alive again. She knows. She just knows. She suppresses the urge to wail. Then her sons disappear and with them the wagon into the dark shroud of night. She hears words but cannot understand them. Whispered voices from the hush that has descended onto the plain.

She looks at Mercy May and says she'll be right back and asks her young daughter to go into the house in case Silas or James Richard should waken. Then she begins to walk after the wagon. For what reason, she cannot tell, other than it feels the right thing to do because when you are married and you love your spouse, you are bound to walk as far as you can with him or her, even over rough terrain, through the bad times, even when he is in a wagon and you are on foot, and you know your footsteps will lead to the brink of death. Mary knows she cannot catch up with the wagon, nor does she want to. She only wants, should a grand accounting sometime take place, to say she walked as far as she could with Arthur until she could walk no farther.

So she begins her walk into the darkness.

She has not gone far before the steady pale light from her house vanishes. But she walks on. The moon is away that night. The only light she can discern comes from stars, cold milky light born maybe millions of years ago that had traveled uninhibited across cosmos to be with her at this time, at this place. And as she walks and thinks and sick worry fills her and floods over, almost as if she was leaving a line of worry behind her in the track; then even the stars seem to fade and their light grows dim. She cannot see the shapes of shrubs or trees along the road and then she can no longer even see the road. The darkness swarms about her and swaddles her, and everything becomes one. It makes no difference whether she walks with her eyes open or closed, because the darkness has taken over, completely and with finality. It provides neither solace nor sorrow, neither softness nor solidity. She is cold and she is empty and she is hungry, but not the kind of hunger that can be assuaged by food.

Mary has become part of the darkness herself.

She vaguely understands that to continue would be pointless, that her duty-offering is acceptable. She has walked as far as she can. She hears a night owl hoot and a rushing through the nearby brush of a small critter, fearful for its life. She sits down and nestles against the trunk of a stubby juniper tree and curls her knees to her chin. She will wait here, wait until she can see again, until the darkness passes, and then she will walk home and hope the morning sun will chase away the blackness. She reminds herself she is still a young woman, and strong. The voices come again, still hushed, the words indecipherable.

She cries, but only a little. She softly says, "Arthur, Arthur, Arthur," and for a few minutes, drifts into a hazy, fretful sleep. When she awakes, she hears the ghostly words spoken, although she is unsure their source. This time, she understands them, and worse, their meaning. The words tell her that when the birds awake, one of them will be missing.

***

So much now is on Lucas's slim shoulders. He rises to the circumstance and rises even more. He knows that some of the patriarchal trust has been ceded to him. He also knows that this night is the most important of his young life and the responsibility he bears is greater than anything he has before experienced. He drives the wagon with an expertise beyond his years. He knows that each bump, each jounce and jar, sends another jolt of agony through his father. Occasionally, he asks Sam, hovering near Arthur in the wagon bed, how their father is faring, and Sam answers, "I don't know. I don't think he's doing all that good, but I don't know. We need to hurry, Lucas. He isn't saying nothing, and his eyes are closed real tight."

In mixture part poise, part grit, Lucas drives on, into town, to the small hospital. He drives the wagon right to the entrance and jumps out and runs into the small office while Sam stays behind and tries to comfort Arthur, who writhes in the wagon bed.

Lucas runs to the first person he comes across, an obese, bristly, pug-faced, fifty-something man named Ferrin Flint. Flint, sitting behind a shabby metal desk. Lucas has seen Flint around town—a fatuous backslapper, a joke teller, red-eyed, smelly, greasy man often with a bottle-shaped bulge hidden under his coat. He is a man with a ready smile, a specious sincerity and a slippery word to everyone. Lucas wonders how he came to be employed at the hospital, even at a menial night-shift job. He is a small man inside a big man's body, wanting to be more than he could ever be.

Flint is the hospital's overnight admitting clerk, the custodian, the shuffler of papers. In the dire situation, Lucas recognizes that he will be dealing with a pompous fool of a man in his attempt to get the medicine that can save his father. Lucas feels woozy as Flint turns toward him, a question forming.

"Son, what's the matter? Why are you here?"

And Lucas explains to him that his father is in the wagon, frightfully ill with tick fever, and he needs help, and he needs it fast.

Flint raises himself from behind the desk with a grunt and says, "Well, let's go outside and see your daddy. You're one of the Bell boys, aren't you? From over near the pole line road?"

Lucas nods and wonders if the faint recognition will help or hinder. Flint walks outside into the cool night and peeks inside the wagon. Flint mumbles and hems and puts his hand on Arthur's forehead and says, although not a physician, "Yep. I'd guess you got it right. Tick fever. He's a mighty sick man."

And Lucas says, "Can we get him inside? Can we get him help? Please, sir."

And Flint says, "How much money you got? Got any at all?"

"No, sir. I don't. We have a little at home, but that's it, and I didn't have time to think about it or take it or anything. We can make it up to you and the hospital and any doctor. We always have paid whatever we owed. I'll be in the Triple C next year; we'll have some money coming in. He needs help. Please."

And the lumbering Flint moves his massive head with the quillish patches of hair, from side to side and says, "No money, no admittance. It's the rules here. I can't break them, because they'd have my job. I can't be of no help."

And at that moment, Lucas understands what pure anger feels like.

"You can do nothing? But this is a hospital. You're supposed to help people here. It's what you do; it's what's right!"

And Flint turns ugly and gets angry and hisses, "You farm people. You don't have anything, but you think you can get whatever you want and pay it off in chicken eggs. We've got enough eggs around here to make omelets until kingdom come, and now you better git. I ain't going to help you. What'd the doctors say in the morning if I took in another dirt-poor clod buster? It'd be my job, and I ain't willing to risk it. Git over to Twin Falls and the hospital there. They have a charity wing, and that's where you and your kind belong. We're done here, young man. Leave! Your daddy's dying and doin' me a favor at the same time."

And he turns his big backside toward the hospital and waddles in. He shakes his head and reaches in a drawer and pulls a bottle out, and when the one other night-shift employee isn't looking, he takes a long hard draw.

Sam, sitting stunned next to his father in the wagon bed says, "What'll we do?"

Lucas, still raging and reeling from Flint's refusal to admit Arthur, fumes. "We go to Twin. It's all we can do. I'll take care of that Flint some other day."

Sam looks at his father, now wan and barely breathing.

"He won't make it, Lucas. Our Daddy will die."

Lucas pulls on the reins and turns around the faithful horse Jenks, points him in the direction of Twin Falls, and again plunges into the night.

***

The Delmar Gray family had left Oklahoma three weeks prior, their destination not quite settled. They left in a small truck with worn tires, a bad radiator, and slappy pistons. It was loaded, even overloaded, and Delmar knew the chances of it making it all the way to Idaho were slim.

But he and his wife, Frances, and their three children had been burned out of their little house by its new owners, a business farm that had no need of a small, dilapidated home, and the Grays barely had time to pack some of their belongings and load them on the wheezy truck and head west. To Idaho. Where a cousin had written that a pulp mill near Lewiston was hiring on graveyard. So off they went, staking their stark future on a scribbled postcard note that had arrived in the mail two months before. The chances were long, the prospects dim. Delmar and Frances knew that. But the Grays had no other options, no other choice.

The old truck did fine for a while. Made it over the Rockies, which came as a relief and a surprise to Delmar, and glided into eastern Utah. Then on to the west and north. Salt Lake City was pleasant, clean, and had more trees than he expected. He turned and went through some of the old pioneer towns then again up and around more mountains—the Black Pines, according to the map he carried in his back pocket, trusting it as though it were a Bible—dry mountains, no streams, no lakes, patches of tough trees huddled on the north slopes. All the while, the old truck seemed to be dying a little more each mile, until it groaned a final time, made a horrible metallic noise, spit out steam, and could run no more. As good luck would have it, a motorist who happened to be a decent mechanic traveled the road soon after the truck sputtered and died, stopped, and asked if he could help. After looking and tinkering with the engine for forty-five minutes, the passerby gave his diagnosis: engine blown up. Won't run again. Useless. Sorry. "Your engine's good for scrap, nothing else," he heavily reported to Delmar and Frances.

They gathered in council. They'd crossed the state line. They were in Idaho. They had a little food, a little money, and their life's belongings.

Delmar said to the Samaritan, "We'll pack up and walk as far as we can. Can you take what we leave behind and keep it somewhere? We can come back for it someday, when we're on our feet and can afford it. If we aren't back in a year, you can keep everything. If we do come back, I'll pay you something for your trouble."

"I guess I can. And I can give you a lift to Albion, if that'll help. It's where I'm headed."

Delmar, Frances, and their three children spent a half hour sifting through their belongings, placing only essentials in a small pile. Delmar had a huge canvas bag with a couple of straps that he'd brought along in case a circumstance such as this should arise. He loaded what he could into the bag, a bit more into two suitcases, and left the rest, along with the useless truck, on the side of the road, relying on a stranger's goodness and word to come back and take care of the rest. The family crowded into the man's vehicle and drove to Albion, where they spent the night under a clump of trees and then began their long walk the following morning.

Delmar hoisted the canvas bag on his shoulders and guessed it weighed 120 pounds. He carried one of the suitcases, Frances the other, and the three children small little bundles of their clothing. That was it.

Lewiston is more than three hundred miles away.

***

Arthur agonizes in the back of the wagon. The pain is rough, hot, and beyond anything he has felt or could imagine. He is dimly aware that he is in a wagon being driven by his two eldest sons. He hears the conversation with the opprobrious Flint but cannot grasp the importance of it. He senses the anger in Lucas, the despair in Sam, the hopelessness of his situation. He does not want the wagon to go farther. He wants it to stop. He wants to rest.

In a brief moment of clarity, he thinks, *So this is what it is like to die.*

All from a tick bite.

He feels darkness all about and then it enters him, small and slow, in his feet and then his legs. It creeps upward. He feels an internal compass turn another way. The searing pain begins to diminish, and in its place, he feels a deep, heavy slumber. The slumber is almost pleasant after the pain he has endured. The blackness climbs higher in his body. He feels heavy, so very heavy. He thinks of Mary and how he will miss her. He considers his sons and figures he's given them enough knowledge and ability to get underway in life. *They'll be okay,* he thinks. *Yes, it will be rough, but they're good boys, and they'll make out fine. Scrappy will help them.* And in this assumption, Arthur is correct; Scrappy will indeed help the boys. The darkness climbs toward his stomach and chest. He feels relieved.

It's over. His thoughts slow and become clumsy. There is no more. Life is ebbing from him, and death is not as horrifying as he once believed. The bumps in the road are no longer noticeable.

The voices of his sons begin to fade and become indistinguishable. Were he able, he would tell them not to worry. He is feeling . . . what . . . what is he feeling? . . . Peace—yes, that's it. Peace and a strange sweetness, something that happens when you finally surrender to the dark feeling snaking up your body, when you just let gravity take hold. The paroxysms of pain are over.

And Mercy May. To think he wanted another son. The joy she brought. Their poems. The way she climbed into his lap at the end of the day. Now, there's something he would like to do again, just once—stretch it out for hours, stretch it out all night. Mercy May, on a calm spring evening, reading poems, telling him about her day at school, as he gently strokes her hair and glories in the sound of her voice. Peace and sweetness, sweetness and peace.

And within him, the darkness comes alive again, creeping once more. Slowly. Steadily. Stealthily. Something in him loosens, then separates, then divides completely.

His thoughts are few. It is as though a coarse black wool blanket has been draped over his body and mind, and he understands it is time to leave. He thinks once more of Mary; then his last breath comes in a little puff, and he is vaguely aware that Sam is crying, and he feels the rage in Lucas, and then, nothing. Nothing more. And the darkness is complete. And so is the peace.

Arthur Bell, true to his character and true to his way, simply steps from one life to the next, with no fanfare, no notice, and no regrets.

***

Arthur died in the early morning hours of a Friday. The services were the following Tuesday. Young Reverend Popplestone, everyone agreed, conducted the funeral and attended to the family with dignity and compassion.

The plates and baskets of food began arriving at the Bell's home within hours after the news of Arthur's death. It was more food than any of the family had ever seen, more food than they could possibly eat themselves. When neighbors came to pay their respects and see how Mary and the children were doing, they were always asked to fill a plate, sit down, and have a bite to eat. And when Mary was timidly asked, "How are you?" she'd always say fine, just fine, because that is all people on the plain would ever say, even when grief had visited and slapped them down. No complaints. No ostentatious "I am well," just and only and simply "fine."

A basket was passed at the services, and envelopes were left anonymously on the Bell's front step. Mary didn't count it all up for a few days, and when she finally got around to it, she was amazed to find that one hundred and sixty-three dollars had been donated to her family.

The sugar bowl was filled again. It overflowed.

Then, a couple of weeks later, she was stunned to find in a rough brown envelope, three one-hundred-dollar bills, no note. This time, the tears came. Mary, who had been successful in holding them back, finally broke down and sobbed right there on her porch, and hoarsely cried across the sagebrush plain for anyone or perhaps no one to hear, "Thank you! Thank you! God bless you!" between her deep wails.

Around a small bend in the road, just out of sight, perhaps a quarter mile from the Bell home, Bowker leaned against an ash tree, listened, and whistled a lonely tune.

***

Two weeks after Arthur's passing, a bright, clean Saturday morning at the Bell home, Mary stirs. She rises up and goes to the corner of the new room, the place where Arthur left the tools.

She finds the hammer, the nails, the saw, the plane. She already has the butcher-paper plans in hand.

Then she walks upstairs to where her sons are sleeping and playfully rubs their shoulders. She is greeted by the same plaintive questions: "Why, Ma? It's so early. It's Saturday, too. Why are you getting us up?"

To which Mary says, "We've got a room to finish."

***

On the very afternoon when the house's new room is completed, on the day when Mercy May will finally get the chance to move her few belongings into it and claim it as her own, on the day when she can at least temporarily brush back the sorrow and mourning of her father's death, there is a knock on the Bell's front door.

Lucas answers it. Before him stands a thin man who looks exhausted, hungry, beat. It is Delmar Gray, who picked the Bell home at random on his long trek toward northern Idaho.

"Pardon, but can I speak with the man of the house?" he shyly asks.

Lucas calls for his mother, who walks slowly to the door, curious.

"Pardon, but me and my family are on foot, trying to get to Lewiston and wondered if we could spend the night under your tree out front and maybe get a little water," Delmar Gray says.

Mary scrutinizes him from toe to head. Not a mean-hearted examination, not with any doubt or skepticism or ill will. She is merely evaluating the lean, tired man and then, behind him, his wife and three raggedy, dust-caked, cracked-skin children. What she sees are five famished, bone-tired people, bound on foot for a place faraway where a better life may or may not be awaiting them. She sees a man and woman who probably haven't eaten in a few days because they have given what scant food they have to their children. She sees a family on the edge of a chasm that they cannot possibly get over. She sees people who are beaten by the times.

Unless there is help.

Mary Bell sees in him and his family a reflection: a reflection of hard times, of sorrow, of grief, of toilsome work with little hope. She sees dead and dying dreams and thoughts of a sweet life sheared away by what people are beginning to call the Great Depression. She sees in the family so much that represents life on the plain in the year 1934. She sees ghosts and hears them calling, ghosts of people gone on, who live only in tired recollection and pulses in the heart. And her heart aches, and she wishes she could make it all better, that things were different—that Arthur would come home from work and want to drive the wagon into town for ice cream, that her children would grow up happy and have enough to get by, that Mercy May would attend college and write her own poems some day, that Scrappy Burroughs would get away from his mountainous pile of debt, that Bowker the madman would find peace. She has a wish for each person on the plain, all of whom are in need of something in some way, as people all over the earth are. She wishes her outlook and wisdom did not come at such a high price. She wishes the world were not so sad and life so wearisome. She wishes there were no refugees, forced from their places by circumstances they cannot control, only people in their homes. She wishes all these things, and then she realizes that happiness for anyone on the plain is not going to come all at once with a swift and mighty change, but will happen gradually with little human kindnesses built one upon the other until, added up, they overreach what only seems to be the insurmountable wall of stone placed in everyone's way by the hard times. Hand over hand, inching up the stone wall, no leaping over it with a lunging single vault. Yes. Yes. That is the way they will overcome; that is the way they will no longer be beat. Kindness. Simple kindness and care and patience.

Delmar Gray stands waiting in an awkward way while Mary's mind whirls in thought, and then, he notices. He is a perceptive man, kind in his core, and notices Mary is dressed in black and there is no man of the house. He notices the subdued children and feels in the room the sorrowful, dull air of recent death. He understands, and even his starving family will not commute his honor. He quietly says, "I'm sorry. You're grieving, and I should have seen it before now. We'll just move along. Thank you anyway. I am truly sorry for your loss, ma'am."

Mary Bell looks at the tattered family, and, even with her own future far from certain, she understands what she must do. She has meat and vegetables from neighbors, fruit from her own cupboard, money passed her way from a hundred hands, a new room never occupied.

She says softly, "No, sir, you may not camp underneath our tree," and Delmar Gray shifts a step backward, and he understands because sorrow is a thick black curtain draped over this household. Then Mary speaks again. "You may come into our house as guests, and we will feed you and take care of you until you are ready to push on. We have a room in our house, newly built, and it will be just right for you and your wife. Circumstances are such that we have more food than we can eat, and we will be happy to share. Stay with us. You would do us honor."

Delmar Gray is a proud man. He has not eaten more than a couple handfuls of flour mixed with water and half a potato in the last three days. His journey ahead is long. He is overwhelmed and embarrassed and cannot help it as the tears form in the corners of his eyes and begin to flow, zagging down the sunburned gullies of his face. Someone has taken the heavy weight from his shoulders. A stranger, at that. He cannot speak. He cannot think of what to say.

But Mary can. She beckons Delmar Gray and simply says, "Please, sir, gather your family and come in."

Chapter Nineteen

THEIR STORIES END THIS WAY, simply told.

Mary Bell houses the Gray family for three days then stuffs enough money into Delmar's quaking hands to buy bus fare to Lewiston, where, miraculously, he finds work at the mill, and the family takes root and beats the hard times. Mary lives another ten years. Her heart, weakened years earlier by rheumatic fever, finally just stops beating shortly after retiring for the night in the home of her eldest son, Lucas. A giant has left.

Lucas serves in the CCC for two years and then joins the army. He sends every paycheck home, which goes a long way toward helping the family through a few more rough years. He makes it through World War II, serves his twenty-year hitch, and then finds work managing a produce company in southeastern Washington. Hard worker, good family man, honorable in every way.

Sam's natural bent for mechanics leads him to work as a plumber, a field in which he excels and prospers, particularly as home-building blossoms after the war. It is always said of Sam that he is a good neighbor and friend, which is all he ever desired.

Silas never strays far from the plain. He works hard, saves his money, and buys a little farm where he raises beets, potatoes, and children. He does all three, friends and family say, very well. His garden is one of the wonders of the valley. He picks up where Arthur's dream falls short, and through him, his father's dream comes true.

James Richard serves in the Navy and much later the Peace Corps, returns, makes it to college where he earns bachelor's and master's degrees and becomes a teacher, then a teacher and principal at a three-room school, then mayor of his little town, and then retires to a small ranch, where he stays until Alzheimer's gets in the way and he is moved to a nursing home in Baker City.

Scrappy Burroughs gets back on his feet, though it takes him many years. With diligence and doggedness, mixed with pure Scottish grit, he tracks down every neighbor who helped him on the morning of the auction, finds out how much money they put down that day, and pays back everyone he could to the penny, plus interest. Scrappy dies at eighty-one, sitting on his porch on a mild spring Saturday evening, listening to his grandchildren and great-grandchildren playing in the yard. He passes in his striped bib overalls with his ancient fedora settled on top of his head. That Scrappy. Now, there was a true man.

And Bowker. He moves back to Colorado a few years after Arthur's death. He comes out of the earth and lives in not much more than a shed in a narrow canyon on the east edge of the Rockies, a thousand feet above where it breaks onto the plain. When the once-in-a-hundred-year cloudburst produces a once-in-a-hundred-year flood in the canyon, the shed and Bowker are both swept away in the mad muddy current. Would-be rescuers toss a thick rope his way, but Bowker seems not to notice and merely tumbles and swashes down the swollen stream, and, according to those who stand on the bank, cackles and waves as he is carried away.

They never could figure the why to Bowker, but the Colorado folk didn't work hard to get to know him, not as hard as his friends in Idaho; they never knew his heart, which was pure and strong because of what he'd suffered. When his body is found two days later snagged high in a cottonwood tree, Bowker's swollen, ruddy mouth is curled into a peaceful smile.

The others, you already know about. The Durhams, the Andrews brothers, Hill Neely's shameful son Edgar, Jo Powell and her boys, Doc Poulsen, and so forth. Big people, mostly, living on a big landscape in small important stories all their own.

Which leaves just one soul, Mercy May.

Hers is not an easy life to describe.

But it goes something like this: She skips two grades and enters high school at twelve. She breezes through high school and thinks about college, but it is never meant to be. There is no money, and a war looms. She enrolls at a secretarial school in Twin Falls and takes room and board from a retired military officer and his wife in return for housekeeping and cooking chores. The officer and his wife are occasionally kind to her. With her secretarial certificate, she decides to leave the plain and takes a job with Farmer's Home in faraway Portland. In a boardinghouse on the northwest side, she meets a dashing sailor, falls in love, and they wed in Seattle while he's on a weekend pass, he in is uniform, she in a simple white dress, sewn by her own hand, that looks vaguely southwestern in style, though the Snake River Plain is as far south as she has ever been.

He ships out. They see each other rarely. She stays in Portland and works at her job and dreams of the man she married and when he will return.

When he does, he is the same but he is different. Too many things have happened to him in the war. He is no longer the confident, happy-go-lucky man she married and sent away. He stays at home for five years. A daughter, then another. He is called to serve in Korea. A son is born while he is at sea. He returns, more morose and frayed than before. A second son comes. And this family settles in, rough years, a few good times, clawing to hold on, to stay together, through the tempests of a confused man who is still at war long after peace is declared. He has seen too much. That's all there is to say. Seen too much.

The children grow, as children are wont to do. Mercy May returns to work to put them through college. The children go away. The husband finally makes peace with himself, then he meets cancer, and the cancer spreads, and his death is agonizing; he stands up one morning, and she hears the bones breaking in his legs and shoulders, and he falls in a heap in terror and pain, and he goes to the hospital and never comes home. At age fifty-two, Mercy May enters widowhood, which she endures for forty years.

She misses him. She loved him. She becomes lonely. She makes the best of things. She reads. At seventy-five, she takes piano lessons and discusses Dostoevsky in her book club, mostly attended by women who didn't make it past the first ten pages of *Crime and Punishment*. Words, words, words, her priceless words. Her story doesn't turn out quite right. No college, a struggle of a marriage, until the very end, when he changed and saw how fortunate he was to have married Mercy May and to have fathered four children who were all good kids.

But even that part of her life, tantalizing and peaceful, ended abruptly when her sailor-husband died. So she endures. She endures. She endures. For forty years, she endures.

She writes poems, but they all become fodder in the fireplace on one particularly rugged night. Her poetry, it turns out, is her life, not ever meant to be words on paper.

***

On a treacherous mountainside just outside of Pendleton, a place called Cabbage Hill, the cell phone call comes as I scream down the highway, wife at my side, the sickness of desperation and of being too late washing over me.

My brother says she failed once during the night. Closed her eyes peacefully and allowed her heart to stop beating. A sister held one hand. A brother-in-law held the other. When her heart stilled, he bent over and kissed her cheek.

Her great heart shuddered, heaved, and started again, and beat for another five hours.

The attending angel of a nurse says she'd never seen such tenderness in the waning moments of anyone's life.

In the end, it's all Mercy May wanted: The chance for her heart to beat once more and, in that hushed, brilliant space, to think of a poem. To let her thoughts flow and soar to people and places from long ago. To bid farewell and wish joy to those nearby. To prepare to meet her sailor again. To know she is loved.

O, sweet Mercy.

About the Author

DONALD SMURTHWAITE WAS BORN IN Portland, Oregon. He now resides in Idaho. He has written nine novels, including *Fine Old High Priests*, *The Boxmaker's Son*, and *Road to Bountiful*. He and his wife, Shannon, are the parents of four children and the overly doting grandparents to four grandchildren. *Sweet Mercy* and its companion booklet, *Sweet Merciful Christmas*, are based on true events that occurred in Idaho during the Great Depression.